SARAH the BOLD

Eileen Lettick

Sarah the Bold

ISBN 978-0-692-18937-5

Published by:
Scribbles 'n Lit

You may write me down in history
With your bitter, twisted lies,
You may trod me in the very dirt
But still, like dust, I'll rise.

-Excerpt from *Still I'll Rise*
By Maya Angelou

For Bob and Marie
Who made it all possible.

E.M.L.

PREFACE

The idea for *Sarah the Bold* began over twenty years ago in my third-grade classroom in Southbury, Connecticut. I was a teacher struggling to find a book to use with a social studies unit I was teaching on Colonial America. After searching and finding nothing that fit the bill, I started to write one. I wrote before school every morning for two and a half years, and as bits of Sarah's story evolved, I shared my work with my students during writing class.

Looking back on those teaching days, I realize that modeling my own writing proved to be the most powerfully authentic writing lessons I ever delivered. My students witnessed their teacher taking risks, being vulnerable, and asking "What if… ?" They watched me make mistakes and cheered me on to completion. As their understanding of author's craft developed, so did mine. I thrived on our writers' share sessions as much as they did.

Over the course of many years and with the help of many students, I fine-tuned Sarah's story and continued to use it as a teaching tool in both writing and social studies. When I retired, I put it on the shelf. A couple of years ago I picked it up again, critiquing it through new eyes, reshaping it, adding a glossary and discussion questions, and preparing it for future readers with the hope that it would someday find a home in classrooms and libraries across the nation. And now, the journey begins.

E.M.L.

CHAPTER 1

"Sarah, are you paying attention?" Mrs. Campbell moved down the aisle toward Sarah's desk. Sarah straightened in her chair and shoved her sketch pad under her social studies book.

"Uh…yes!"

"Really?" Mrs. Campbell said, narrowing her eyes. "What was I just talking about while you were doodling?"

"Uh, the American Revolution?"

"What specifically?" Mrs. Campbell folded her arms across her chest and tapped her foot.

Sarah shrugged. "I don't know."

"The Stamp Act of 1765. It was one of the issues that led up to the American Revolution. The British Crown taxed every document in the colonies." The teacher sighed.

"It may be your birthday, Sarah, but there's a test Monday, and I hope you'll be prepared." Sarah looked down at her desk as the bell rang.

"Remember class, your papers on Colonial America are due next Wednesday," Mrs. Campbell called out over the clamor of fifth graders chatting and packing up to leave.

"Mrs. Campbell's cool, but I don't know why she thinks the American Revolution's such a big deal," Sarah said, as she boarded the school bus with Julia and Karen.

"Yeah, who cares? It's not as if we don't know how it turned out," Julia said. The girls giggled.

"So, you think you're getting those roller blades, Sarah?" Karen asked.

"Yup, I saw the box in my father's study. Perfect shape. Perfect size." Sarah grinned.

"Great! Pretty soon the Rockin' Rollers will be zooming around Meadow Drive," Julia said.

"And I can't wait," Sarah smiled.

Sarah sprinted off the school bus and ran down Meadow Drive. She passed her dad's car in the driveway and flew up the front steps. Dad had rescheduled his patients to come home early, and Mom had stayed home from her book club meeting. Sarah raced through the front door.

"Happy Birthday!" her family shouted. Green crepe paper and pink balloons hung from the chandelier in the dining room. Sarah grinned as her parents and five-year-old brother, Jerome, wearing hot pink party hats, swooped in for a group hug.

Sarah grinned and politely sat through the birthday song, a pinch-to-grow-an-inch, and the cutting of the chocolate devils-food cake that dripped with loads of pink and green frosting. Jazzy lime-green letters spelled out her name, and eleven gold candles surrounded a first-place swimming medal made with thin wisps of blue and gold frosting.

Sarah could hardly contain herself when her father pulled out the bright green package with the soft pink bow. "Can I open it now?"

"Not so fast, my pretty. First, your old man wants a little sugar." Her father pulled her toward him. He yanked one of her dark braids, pinched her nose, and then planted a sloppy wet one on her cheek. With deep brown eyes twinkling, he held the box in front of her.

She imagined herself whizzing around the neighborhood sporting her new, neon purple, inline skates; the ones that she had seen in The Sports Center's window.

Even her little brother, Jerome, twitched with excitement. His chubby brown fingers reached for the package.

"Let me help, Sarah." Jerome never cared what was in the gift as long as he was able to open it.

"This one's all mine, little brother," Sarah said, as she pulled the box towards her.

Shock and disappointment shot through her as soon as she held the package. It was the right size, but the wrong weight! *Oh no!* she thought. She yanked off the pink bow and green wrapping paper and tore the box open. She rummaged through layers of pink tissue paper. Nestled inside was the oddest-looking doll Sarah had ever seen. A round wooden head attached to a flimsy cloth-stuffed body was all there was to it. Two painted black dots for eyes stared at her over a half-moon smile. A tiny cloth bonnet covered its head, and a scarlet cloak hid half a plain, calf-length, blue aproned dress. On the doll's wrist was a white tag bearing her father's handwriting, "To Sarah, with love."

Sarah's heart raced, and her ears rang as her father rambled on about how the doll was a real find. "I bought it at old man Langley's store. He said it's very rare... an antique... a colonial poppet made in the eighteenth century... said to have been owned by a woman who performed magic... I thought it would be a great addition to your collection."

Blah, blah, blah. Colonial poppet! Who cares! Sarah thought. Sarah searched her father's face, expecting him to burst out laughing and pull out her real gift. "But Daddy? Where are my rollerblades?"

Her father glanced over at her mother and then back to Sarah and sighed. "Sweetheart, there aren't any. Coach says—"

"Coach says? What does *he* know?" Sarah's eyebrows shot up and her almond-shaped eyes filled with tears. "Daddy, you knew I was planning on skates. You practically promised me."

Her father's voice echoed in her ears. "Coach said that it wouldn't be wise for you to rollerblade until after the championship swim meet. He said that you could fall and put yourself out of the competition, and he's relying on you to win the state championship. He said you're the next Simone Manuel."

"It's not fair! I don't want to wait until after the swim meet. My birthday's today, and I deserve those rollerblades now! You said—"

"I said when the final swim meet was over we'd discuss it."

Sarah's jaw dropped. She could feel her face flush as she fought back the tears. "I don't want another doll. I'm not a baby!"

Sarah's mother cleared her throat and stood up. She glared at her daughter. "Young lady, you had better watch your tone and thank your father."

Sarah looked at her mother and then back at her father.

"All the other kids at school have roller blades. Besides, I already told Julia and Karen that I *knew* I was getting them." As she burst into tears, she grabbed the doll, ran to her room, and slammed the door.

Hours later, Sarah continued to sulk in her room. She opened the window and stared at the night sky, ignoring the stream of texts on her cell phone from friends who anxiously awaited her description of the perfect birthday gift she never received. A cool breeze wafted into the room. She scowled at her swimming trophies that told the story of her star performances over the past five years—best breaststroke, strongest butterfly, and most accomplished junior freestyle. The trophies and her doll collection occupied all of the space on her lavender painted wooden shelves. *Swimming is getting in the way of me being cool*, she thought.

The grins from her stuffed animals, perched on her pink and green comforter, taunted her; while the eyes of Justin Beiber and Beyonce posters, on the wall, cast mocking looks. *What will the girls say when I tell them? I should have picked it up and shaken it when I discovered it the other day. Tomorrow, I'll have to tell all my friends what happened,* she thought.

"And you!" She lifted the doll and stared into its eyes. "This is all your fault!" Sarah looked over at the others so lovingly displayed. "You don't belong with them." Sarah tossed the poppet onto her bed.

The doll bounced across the thick comforter and landed face down.

Sarah's eyes rested on Addie, her favorite American Girl doll. Her mother often remarked how much Sarah resembled Addie with her tight braids, broad nose, and full lips. She loved Addie, her only doll with skin as brown as her own.

Sarah walked over to the bed and picked up the new doll. She held her at arm's length.

"You're a pickle puss with those tiny eyes and that smile. And I have the perfect name for you—Miss Prickle! After Daddy forgets about you, I'll put you in the closet."

The doll replied with a hollow stare.

"I'm sorry I ever signed up for swimming lessons! I wish I lived someplace where there were no swimming pools or coaches!" Sarah hurled the poppet against the bedroom door. Crack! As the doll's wooden head banged against the door frame, Sarah fell. A flash of bright white light and a shrill buzzing in her ears were the last recollections she had before darkness crashed around her.

* * *

"Wake up, child," came a gruff voice. "Are you dead?"

Is it morning already? Sarah wondered. *Why is Daddy waking me? I didn't hear the alarm.*

"I don't want to get up," Sarah rolled over.

"On your feet, child!" Startled at the sound of an unfamiliar voice, Sarah opened her eyes. Looming above her stood a burly man in a strange outfit. A tri-cornered black hat covered his full white wig, and he wore a tattered, long, dark coat. On his feet was a pair of scuffed black shoes with tarnished brass buckles. In one hand he held a glowing lantern that illuminated his face. In his other hand, he held a thick stick. He poked her. "On your feet, child!"

"W-W-What?" Sarah stared up at the man. "Who are you?"

"I'm Jacob Dredge, the town watchman, and this settlement does not tolerate runaway servants. Now, where are your quarters?"

"I-I-I don't understand. What's going on?" She shivered and reached for her jacket pockets. There were no pockets. "Where's my jacket? What's this?" she said, looking at her clothes and finding herself dressed in a blue, calf-length, aproned dress and a scarlet cloak. She lifted the front panel of her outfit. "I'm dressed like that doll! Where's my bedroom? Where *am* I?"

Frantic, she raised her hands to her head. Her fingers slid over a tight cloth cap. "Ouch!" She winced when she discovered a large bump on the crown of her head. "What's going on, mister? Why are we dressed like this?" Sarah said, motioning to their outfits.

"Do not be rude to me, girl, I'll—."

"But I didn't mean to—"

Dredge grabbed Sarah's arm. "I'll find your master and have you thrashed!"

Sarah twisted and pulled her arm free. "My master? I don't have a ... Where's my bedroom? Where are my parents? Where am I?" Sarah whimpered.

"Where are your quarters, child!" Dredge bellowed.

Sarah's body stiffened as her eyes darted in every direction. *Am I dreaming?* she wondered. She stared at Dredge.

"Well, child, are you going to tell me where your quarters are or not? Out with it! I have my rounds to make!"

"W-W-Where am I? I was in my bedroom, and now... and now *you're* here. This can't be happening. Stuff like this doesn't happen." Sarah shook her head back and forth in disbelief. "If this is a dream, I need to wake up, now!"

Dredge threw back his shoulders and put his hands on his hips. "In the name of King George and all the good settlers of Guilford, I command you to declare your quarters!"

"Huh?" Sarah rose, unsteady on her feet. "My quarters? I don't have any money, mister," she said as she backed away from him and held out upturned palms. Dredge leaned forward and gave her a menacing look.

"Now wait, mister, we can figure this out. There's no need to—" Sarah backed up. "Just keep away from me."

A dark scowl crossed the watchman's face. "Stubborn, eh? I'll waste no time with a runaway. Your master will deal with you on the morrow, and I will enjoy seeing you thrashed. Now move!" He grabbed her collar and shoved her forward.

Sarah stumbled. "Stop it! Get your hands off me! Somebody, call the police! Ahhhh!" Sarah screamed at the top of her lungs and began to run.

The watchman lunged, dropped his club, scooped her up with one hand, and planted her firmly on his hip.

"Put me down! Somebody, help me!" Sarah kicked and screamed. She grabbed at the watchman's face and hair and pushed his wig down onto his forehead. When his right hand came up to protect himself, Sarah sunk her teeth into it.

"Ooh!" Dredge yanked his hand away. "So, you want to be treated like a dog, eh!" Dredge smacked her across her right ear and flung her onto the ground. After tugging his hair back into place, he grabbed his club and charged at her.

Thwack! Crack! Dredge smashed Sarah's shoulder. She jumped backward, and he swung again. She ducked and covered her head.

"Help! Someone, help me!"

The watchman sneered. "No one is going to help you! No one would dare!" Dredge scrunched up his face and tore Sarah's cap off her head. He grabbed a fistful of her hair and yanked hard.

Sarah screamed louder.

"Now, you'll be coming with me," he said through clenched teeth. Dropping his lantern, he grabbed Sarah's hair with his left hand. With his other, he jabbed and prodded her forward with his club.

CHAPTER 2

Thud! Thud! Thud! Dredge pounded on the heavy oak door. It opened with a prolonged squeak. There stood a thin, silver-haired man, with soft, brown eyes peering through wirerimmed eyeglasses. He sported a long, dark bathrobe, and his two large ears fanned out from under a wrinkled, cream-colored nightcap.

The winded watchman dropped Sarah on the doorstep and stood over her. "Reverend Ruggles, my apologies for disturbing you at this hour."

"Why, Mr. Dredge?" The Reverend looked from the watchman to Sarah and back again.

"What is the matter?"

"On your feet!" Dredge snarled. When Sarah didn't budge, he shoved his foot under her thigh and forced her across the threshold. Holding tight to Sarah's shoulder, Dredge removed his hat. "I came upon this runaway sleeping on the village common. She won't offer the whereabouts of her master. Would you kindly lock her in the stable for the night and I will return for her on the morrow when the jail opens?"

Sarah's jaw dropped. "What?" she said.

"Jacob, certainly there is no need to lock the child up with the animals. I'll have Bridget prepare a sack. She can bed down in the kitchen."

Wide-eyed with disbelief, Sarah blurted out, "I'm not staying here and sleeping in your kitchen. Where's my cell phone? I'm calling my parents."

Dredge and Reverend Ruggles exchanged questioning looks.

"What is a cell phone?" the Reverend said.

"You know. A phone. Ring-a-ling?" Sarah gestured with her hand to her ear. Her heart raced. "Please, Reverend, I can't stay here. Let me use your phone. I want to go home." Sarah started to cry. Dredge glared at her and tightened his grip. Reverend Ruggles shot a look at the watchman holding fast to Sarah.

"Really, Mr. Dredge, I think you needn't—" The preacher raised his eyebrows.

"He hit me with his club, Reverend, really! I want my parents!" Sarah writhed under Dredge's grip.

The watchman released his hold, and his face turned red. "She's complaining of a bump on her head. It's clear that the girl is addled."

"Ah yes," the minister nodded. "I'll handle this, Mr. Dredge." Reverend Ruggles ushered a sobbing Sarah into his study while Dredge followed. Sarah collapsed into a highbacked, oak chair.

"Oh, and before it escapes me," Dredge said. He yanked Miss Prickle out of his pocket.

"I found *this* on the ground beside her." Sarah stared at the doll. Dredge handed the poppet to Reverend Ruggles. Shaking his head, the watchman muttered, "Imagine, a white-faced poppet for a brown-faced servant girl. No doubt it's stolen."

"I didn't steal that doll! She's mine!"

"We will see about *that*." Dredge sneered at Sarah.

While the men moved toward the front door and continued speaking, Sarah looked around the dimly lit room. A fireplace, with gray, rounded stones, covered one wall from floor to ceiling. A few dying embers drifted across a cobbled hearth. Before a small window stood a wide oak desk with a quill pen in a square, green glass inkwell. A small lamp emitted a subtle scent of oil and cast a soft glow across an open leather-bound

Bible. A brown, braided, oval rug covered knotty pine floorboards.

Sarah turned with a start as the mantel clock struck 11:30 pm. She placed her hands over her face and closed her eyes. *What has happened to me? This doesn't make sense,* Sarah thought. *Could it be...a class field trip to a museum... I missed the bus... left behind with the acting staff. That's it! But why are they still here?* Tears slid down her face. At the sound of approaching footsteps, she raised the corner of her apron and blotted her face dry. She took a deep breath. *Okay, I need to get a grip and stay strong to figure this out,* she thought.

"Well, have you had a chance to ponder your circumstances?" Reverend Ruggles stood before her holding Miss Prickle.

Sarah looked at the floor.

"What's your name?" He studied her face. "What's your pretty poppet's name?" He slowly handed her the doll.

"My name's Sarah and the doll's name is... Miss Prickle."

The Reverend smiled. "Very good, Sarah, and how old are you?"

"Eleven"

"Hmm." The Reverend stroked his chin. "And wouldn't you and Miss Prickle like to go home?"

"Yes!" Sarah nodded and smiled up at the preacher.

"Good. Then let me help."

"Great! I know my parents must be going nuts by now."

Reverend Ruggles furrowed his brow. "Your speech, you don't speak as though you are from around here, and not at all like a servant."

"I'm *not* a servant."

"Hmm. Well, how did you get here?" he whispered.

"That's what *I'd* like to know. Today's my birthday, and I was in my bedroom and… " Sarah looked at the floor and slowly shook her head.

The preacher squinted at her over his glasses. "Yes, well, you've had quite a mishap. I will awaken Mrs. Ruggles and ask her to lay out a sack for you. I think its best that you get some rest, and we will talk in the morning."

"Reverend, this can't wait. Call the security guard; he'll take me home. I don't wanna sleep over." She folded her arms across her chest.

Reverend Ruggles pursed his lips and glared at Sarah. "Although it is evident you are confused, you exhibit behavior unlike anything I have experienced from a young girl or servant before. No doubt this is the reason you have been beaten and left on the common. I do not condone your mistreatment, but it is understandable that a Negro your age would be disciplined for such intolerable speech and attitude. As for your demand to summon a guard, you have already met the only security the settlement of Guilford has. By my observations, you will not want to confront Mr. Dredge again this evening." The preacher shook his finger at Sarah. "Now, stay put, and I will get my wife." He heaved a long sigh, turned and climbed the narrow staircase.

Sarah heard footsteps and a creak from the wooden staircase. Reverend Ruggles and a prim-looking, slender woman in a long, brown robe entered the room. A white gown peeked out from under the robe, and a lacy nightcap hugged her head. One long, thin, gray braid cascaded down her back and round wire-rimmed glasses rested on her large nose. In her tiny hands, she carried a short, lit candle. Mrs. Ruggles reminded Sarah of Old Mother Hubbard.

"Good evening, child," said Mrs. Ruggles.

Reverend Ruggles pulled a high-backed bench from in front of the fire.

"What is your name?" she asked, inspecting Sarah with her steely, gray eyes.

"Sarah Osborne."

"Sarah Osborne? Why that's not a proper name for a slave. Now tell me the truth."

Sarah frowned. "Mrs. Ruggles, that really *is* my name."

"Well then, Sarah Osborne, for what family are you a servant?"

"I'm *not* a servant. I'm Louis and Ella Osborne's daughter, and I don't want to play make-believe anymore. I just want to go home!" Sarah stomped her foot and bit her lip to fight back the tears.

"You cannot even hope to solve your problem with such brazenness, child. Now tell me, where is your home?"

"213 Meadow Drive, Guilford, Connecticut."

Reverend and Mrs. Ruggles exchanged glances.

"This *is* the settlement of Guilford, but there is no Meadow Drive, nor are there Osbornes. It appears you are being dishonest with me, Sarah; therefore, you are most likely a runaway. The law requires that we seek your rightful owners."

Sarah froze. She stared into the two elderly faces. "No! No! This can't be! This stuff can't happen!" She moaned, shaking her head. Sarah dreaded the answer to the question she knew she needed to ask. She inhaled a long, deep breath, leaned forward in her chair, and tightly gripped its arms. "What's t-t-today's date?" She squeezed her eyes shut.

"Why it is the eighteenth of April, child, 1765."

Sarah let out her breath, opened her eyes wide and groaned. She tried to stand, but her legs wouldn't hold her. She gulped in air. "I can't… It's so hot in here." She clawed at her cloak and the high neckline of her dress. "I can't breathe. Get this off me. I feel so… " Sarah slapped her hand across her mouth to try to contain what was sure to erupt any second. Her eyes darted around the room and searched in vain for a wastebasket. As Sarah lifted her cloak and formed a large, red trough, she exploded in loud, wet and rancid heaves.

Mrs. Ruggles stepped back, and the Reverend fled the room. He watched from the doorway as Sarah struggled to contain heave after heave of vomit. When the lumpy, sticky, smelly contents of her stomach had filled up the folds of her cloak, she ended with one final, loud belch and a whimper.

Mrs. Ruggles scurried into the kitchen for a wet rag, and when she returned she draped it over the straight-back chair. She unbuttoned Sarah's cloak, bunched it up on the ends, folded it inward and then handed it to her husband. "Thomas, please take this to the well and wash it." She handed the rag to Sarah who mopped up her face and patted her lips.

"There, there, child. Are you feeling better?" Mrs. Ruggles brushed the hair from Sarah's face.

"Yes." She held out the soiled rag. "What should I do with this?"

Mrs. Ruggles led her to the back door. "Leave it there on the step. My husband will dispose of it. Go to the study and undress. I will bring you some bedding and a gown." Mrs. Ruggles headed back up the staircase.

Sarah cried as she loosened the buttons on her dress. Through her tears, she spotted Miss Prickle sitting on the desk staring at her. She picked up the doll and pressed her face into the folds of the doll's dress. "Miss Prickle, how did we get here?" She sniffled. "And how do we go home?

CHAPTER 3

Sarah awoke to the crow of a rooster. Her eyes were sore and swollen, and her body ached. Although the savory smells of beef and muffins filled the air, she had no appetite. She peeked between her quilt and stuffed muslin sack and spotted Mrs. Ruggles preparing breakfast. *Oh no, the old lady! How can I face her after throwing up last night?* she thought.

Sarah cringed as she remembered the last time she had thrown up like that. She had been in first grade. Her entire class had watched and held their noses while Mrs. Ellis had to scrape the vomit off her shoes. Sarah had excused herself and hid in the bathroom until her mother picked her up.

"Good morning!" A cheery voice interrupted Sarah's thought. A freckled-faced girl with a full head of long, red ringlets and large, sparkling green eyes bent down next to her. Sarah judged the girl to be a couple of years younger than she.

"Huh? Oh, hi," Sarah said.

"I am Anna. I live here, and you are Sarah Osborne."

THEY have a kid? Sarah thought.

"I know all about you. You are eleven years. You fell and hit your head, and now you are addled."

"Anna! That will be enough."

"Yes, Grandmother." The girl turned back to Sarah and whispered, "Do not worry, Sarah Osborne." She stroked Sarah's forehead. "We will find your family."

I hope you're right, she thought.

"Grandmother and I will take you to Mr. Hill today. He will know who your master is. He registers all the new settlers, even those simply passing through."

"Breakfast is almost ready, Anna," Grandmother said. "Sarah, your garments are warming near the fire. Make haste, child!"

Sarah slid out from beneath the covers. Self-conscious in the ill-fitting gown, she reached for the quilt to cover herself.

Anna laid the cover on a chair and then reached for the crumpled sack. Nestled in one of the deep folds lay Miss Prickle. Sarah scooped her up.

"What a lovely poppet! What is her name?"

"Um...Miss Prickle."

"Why, that's a curious name."

Sarah shrugged.

"Anna, show Sarah to your chamber. She can dress and wash there. I will store the bedding," Mrs. Ruggles said.

The girls gathered up Sarah's clothes and climbed the narrow staircase. Anna entered a small room. Sarah stopped at the doorway. Her large brown eyes scanned the bedroom.

Anna's bedroom contained a small cradle with a doll, a wooden trundle bed, and a large trunk. On top of the trunk was a tin panel with tiny holes punched into it spelling out A-N-N-A. Surrounding her name were miniature acorns.

Sunlight streamed through a small window onto the cradle which held a worn blonde doll in a faded green velvet dress. Anna picked up the doll and cuddled her. "Her name is Clarisse. She was my mother's."

"Does your mother live here, too?"

"No, Mother died of smallpox, nine years ago, shortly after I was born. I don't remember her." Anna cast expressive eyes toward Sarah.

"Oh, I'm sorry. What about your father?"

"Father went off to fight the French four years ago and never returned. Grandmother and Grandfather are my only family now."

Sarah looked down at the floor. "Oh no. I don't know what I'd do if…but do you remember your father?"

"Oh, yes." Anna smiled. "Father was a cabinetmaker. He always smelled of pine and cedar. He used to throw me up on his shoulders and carry me through the village when he made his rounds. Father called me his "Little Acorn." Before he left, he fashioned this trunk for me." Anna walked over to the trunk at the foot of the bed and ran her fingers across the lid.

Sarah smiled and glanced around the room. "You sure are neat. Is all your stuff in the trunk?"

"Stuff?" Anna gave Sarah a blank stare.

"Your stuffed animals, books and toys?"

"These *are* all my belongings, Sarah. You have seen my poppet. The only animals we have are kept in the barn, and we read from Grandfather's Bible every night. We must leave our primers at the schoolhouse. It is a disappointment."

"What are primers?"

"The books we read."

"So, if you're not allowed to bring your books home, then that means no homework? I wouldn't mind *that* disappointment."

Anna cocked her brow. "I find your speech strange. You don't speak like you are from this region."

That's because it's 1765 and I haven't even been born yet! I wonder if I am really real, Sarah thought. She pinched her arm. Sarah poked her head into the hallway. "Anna, I need to use your bathroom."

"Bathroom?" We bathe only on Saturday."

"Then where's your toilet?"

"Toilet?"

"Anna, I need to go!" Sarah leaned in and crossed her legs."

"Oh dear! You must forgive me. I have already cleaned my chamber pot. I must ask you to use the outside privy."

Outside? Oh, no! Just like Camp Happy Horizons and those smelly outhouses that the counselors made us use, Sarah thought. She straightened up. "Uh, I'll wait."

Anna lifted the pitcher, poured water into the bowl on the dresser and handed Sarah a damp cloth. "Following the morning meal, Grandmother will give you some anise paste with which to freshen your mouth."

Sarah nodded.

"I'll leave you to your dressing. Grandmother will need me to place the trenchers on the table for breakfast."

"Trenchers? What are they?"

"Wooden dishes. We only have three, so you and I will need to share. I know they are very common," Anna lowered her eyes, "but Grandmother reserves the good china for Christmas and Easter." Anna walked over to her dresser. "You may use my horsehair brush and looking glass. When you are dressed, do join us." Anna smiled and scampered downstairs.

Sarah removed the nightgown and folded it carefully and laid it on Anna's bed. She picked up the worn blue dress and held it close to absorb the warmth it still held from hanging so close to the fire. Her fingers fumbled over small hooks that started at the back of her neck and went down her spine. She secured the apron with a bow at her waist, put on the same stockings she had worn the night before, and laced up the worn, brown shoes. Now she was dressed like Anna, except that Anna's gray dress and crisp white apron were in much better condition. Sarah looked in the mirror, smoothed out the part in her hair with the soft bristles of Anna's brush and straightened her braids. The last item of clothing was the white cap. Sarah picked it up and considered it. *Anna and her grandmother wear these in the house. I have no idea why, but it must be the thing to do around here,* Sarah thought.

After she slid the cap onto her head and tied the straps into a bow, she made a funny face at herself in the mirror. Grabbing Miss Prickle, she headed to the kitchen.

"She's a runaway, Bridget!"

At the sound of Dredge's booming voice, Sarah stopped midway down the stairs.

"It is my obligation as a respected, duly appointed official to report her. A runaway does not deserve a morning meal!"

Sarah tiptoed further down the stairs and stopped on the last step. She held her breath and peeked into the kitchen.

"Jacob, Jacob, Jacob," Mrs. Ruggles said, shaking her head. "She is but a child. Where is your compassion? *She* is God's creature, too!"

"She's a Negress!"

Sarah gasped and bit her lip.

"Jacob Dredge, your position as town watchman does not give you the authority to treat people poorly. Brown or white, no child will go without breakfast in the home of Bridget Ruggles. 'Suffer the little children to come to me,' Jacob. Isn't that what the Good Book says?"

You tell 'em, Mrs. Ruggles! Sarah thought.

"Hmph! That does not include *her* kind." Dredge scowled.

Mrs. Ruggles slid a wrought iron pot filled with dough across the hearth into the brick oven. "Thomas will be in from the barn presently. You may either join us *all* for breakfast, and then take the child to Nathaniel Hill, or you may go on your way, and I will tend to it."

"You will *not* have that girl share the same table with you!"

Grandmother's whole body stiffened. "It is time for you to take your leave, Mr. Dredge."

"You won't be speaking so high and mighty after I tell Nathaniel Hill about this. The parson's wife or not, a woman should speak to me with more respect!"

Anna stared with wide eyes and mouth agape.

Dredge slammed the door and stormed off.

"Grandmother, Mr. Dredge seems so angry! What will he do? What will Grandfather say?"

Mrs. Ruggles chuckled. "Don't fret, dear. That dog's bark is worse than his bite. Now go fetch Sarah."

As Anna stood up, Sarah appeared in the doorway and smiled. "I'm here, Mrs. Ruggles, and thank you." The woman nodded.

"Good morning, good women." Reverend Ruggles whooshed through the door and smiled, his face ruddy from the outdoors. Mrs. Ruggles smiled back.

"Grandfather, Mr. Dredge came to take Sarah and—"

"Hush, child. Both of you, take a seat."

At their small oak table, Mrs. Ruggles, Anna, and Sarah bowed their heads as Reverend Ruggles led them in prayer. "Merciful Father, we thank Thee for the food you have provided. Please guide us in sharing Your love, compassion, and kindness with others. Bless my good wife, Bridget, my dear granddaughter, Anna, and Sarah Osborne, whom You have laid on our doorstep. As always, I remain Your servant and pray for Your divine guidance. Amen."

"Amen," the women answered.

CHAPTER 4

After breakfast, Anna led Sarah to the outside privy. When the girls returned, Mrs. Ruggles announced that she would accompany them across the common to the office of Mr. Nathaniel Hill, the Clerk of the Settlement.

"No doubt Jacob Dredge has already reported to Nathaniel," Grandmother muttered as she centered her granddaughter's apron. "Anna, you have removed your coif once again. Certainly, a poor example for Sarah. Why your dear mother, may God rest her soul, would never forgive me if she knew how much you have freckled."

Anna bowed her head. "Sarah Osborne, I displease Grandmother so when I do not shade my cheeks. I am afraid my fiery hair and spotted face are a constant embarrassment to her. I am forever applying horseradish and warm milk to my freckles, but they never disappear. When I get older, I shall be forced to blacken my hair if I ever expect a gentleman to call."

"I daresay, Anna, you dwell on your appearance too much. You know what the Good Book teaches about vanity!" Grandmother said. She reached over and nudged an errant burning ember back into the fire.

Gentlemen callers? She's nuts! Boys are gross! Sarah thought. A pang of guilt shot through her. *Not Jerome, though! I'd give anything to hear the irritating sound his lips make when his pudgy hand pushes one of his matchbox cars across the kitchen floor.*

"We must take our leave. Sarah, kindly refrain from moping!" Mrs. Ruggles said.

Sarah fastened her cloak. She glanced at Miss Prickle seated on the kitchen chair and then scooped her up. *Should I bring you along or not? I don't want people to think I'm a baby. I dunno, and what if someone says I stole you?* Sarah looked into Miss Prickle's face. *No, you'll be safer here.* She placed the doll back on the chair.

As the trio crossed the green, Sarah took in her vaguely familiar surroundings. *Where's the restaurant? It's gone! No, it hasn't been built yet! This is too weird!* Sarah thought, when she didn't see The Cornerstone Restaurant where her mother used to take her after swim practice. She took a deep breath and smiled. *I can still smell those juicy burgers dripping with creamy sauce. And those fries were the best! I wonder if Anna has ever tasted French fries.* Sarah's mouth watered.

Instead of The Sports Center, there stood only three tiny gray houses. *None of the stores that I know exist yet, but somehow, I exist. I just don't get this,* Sarah thought, shaking her head.

To the left, sheep and cows grazed in the sunlight next to a cemetery. Sarah dodged large puddles and stepped around small gravestones that peeked above the overgrown grass. This was so unlike the beautifully manicured green she knew with its clean, concrete sidewalks and stately flagpole. The pink and gray granite Civil War Soldier Monument was missing, and in its place was a tall post with thick rope handcuffs.

"Hey, Anna, what's that?" Sarah pointed.

"You know what that is, Sarah Osborne," Anna said, smiling.

"No, I don't," Sarah said.

"Everyone knows what that is!"

"Just tell me."

"The whipping post, silly."

"Do they beat the animals?"

"No, that is where Mr. Hill flogs those who do not keep the law."

"How cruel," Sarah whispered.

"It is his duty." Anna looked away.

Sarah stood before a small stone church surrounded by poplar trees. To the right, stood a white steepled church with a huge clock bearing golden Roman numerals. It resembled the Congregational Church she attended, but to the left, there was no sign of Jefferson's Market where her mother bought sticky buns every Sunday morning. Maggie's Dress Shoppe and the Lanowitz Deli were also missing. Just a few, small brown houses stared back at her.

Sarah stumbled over her long cloak. "Keep up, child," Mrs. Ruggles said, without breaking her stride. Sarah longed for the comfort of her sneakers and jeans, while she wondered what Mr. Dredge had told Mr. Hill. She hoped the clerk would be more understanding. Mrs. Ruggles stopped at a slate gray, one-story house and knocked on the door.

The door opened and there stood Nathaniel Hill, a round, dark-haired man with plump, pink cheeks. His wire-rimmed glasses sat low on his nose. "Well, good morning, good women. Please come in. I must say I am surprised to have callers so early."

"Good morning, Nathaniel. No doubt Jacob Dredge has been to call already, so I'm certain that he has told you of the Negress who calls herself Sarah Osborne." As Mrs. Ruggles pointed toward her, Sarah's stomach fluttered.

"Indeed, he has. And I must say there has been no report of a runaway servant, except for a male. It was noted and posted a fortnight ago." Mr. Hill pointed a meaty finger at the wall.

Mrs. Ruggles and Anna glanced at the wall, but Sarah walked over to the posting.

MISSING
Male Negro Runaway
Belonging to Caleb Johnson
Stole Loaf of Bread and Two Fish
Return for Public Thrashing

Uh oh, he better hope Mr. Dredge doesn't catch up with him, Sarah thought.

A faded black and white drawing of a snake, cut into eight pieces, hung on the dusty wall. Each piece had an abbreviation above it. Under the snake were the words "JOIN OR DIE." Sarah recognized it from her social studies book but couldn't recall what it meant. On another wall were postings of public meetings, church services and a list of townspeople seeking to exchange goods for farm animals. Sarah read a notice torn from the *Connecticut Courant.*

> The last Tuesday of this month
> (being the 23rd day)
> there is to be a General Congress of the
> Sons of Liberty of this colony
> to meet in New Haven.

The Sons of Liberty! Wow! Sarah remembered her class play— the Boston Tea Party. Joseph Cook and Gerald Oakley, their faces painted black and dressed as Mohawk Indians, screamed as they threw crates of tea into the Boston Harbor to protest the British taxes.

"Come closer, Missy," Mr. Hill said.

Sarah took a few steps closer.

"It would not be just to punish you until we establish what wrong you have done. Until your rightful master makes an inquiry, you will be quartered at the parsonage and will take on the duties required of a servant in the employ of the Reverend and Mrs. Ruggles. Is that clear?"

Sarah swallowed hard and took a deep breath. "Mr. Hill, something very strange has happened. I d-d-don't belong here, at least not in this time. I'm not a servant in someone's household. I'm an ordinary girl with parents and a little brother. I go to school every day, and I've read about this time period in books. I need to get back home to my parents. Please help me."

"A Negress attending a schoolhouse? Why that's preposterous! I will not stand for any of your lies! Mrs. Ruggles, if you will excuse me, I have much work to do."

"Come along, child, and stop this foolishness." Mrs. Ruggles grabbed Sarah's arm and headed for the door.

Sarah pulled away. "Look, I'll prove it!" She leaped over to the pictures and postings and read "Join or die! And here Mr. Johnson wants his slave returned. He stole two fish and a loaf of bread."

Mrs. Ruggles strode over to Sarah. "Shush, child!" she said, placing her hand over Sarah's mouth, but Sarah pulled away.

"And this one tells of a meeting of the Sons of Liberty on the 23rd! They're probably going to discuss the Stamp Tax. You know, 'no taxation without representation.' So there, Mr. Hill! I *can* read, and I *do* know what's going on. And my parents have taught me never to lie!"

As Sarah's nostrils flared, Anna and Mrs. Ruggles stared at her, stone-faced.

The clerk leveled an indignant glare at Mrs. Ruggles. "Bridget, I'll not have this in my office! Did this girl learn about these things in *your* home?"

"Of course not, Nathaniel! We only speak of religion in *my* home. It is certain she is addled; surely Mr. Dredge reported this! I do so apologize for her behavior. This won't happen again. I will bring her back to the parsonage and give her a good thrashing!"

"A thrashing? For what? *Reading*?" Sarah said.

Mrs. Ruggles gasped and pressed her index finger to her lips.

Mr. Hill peered over his glasses. In controlled, low tones that sent a chill down Sarah's spine, he moved closer. "No. I prefer to deal with this one myself." When he closed in on Sarah, she scampered behind his chair.

"But I didn't *do* anything!" she cried.

"Oh dear." Mrs. Ruggles said, wringing her hands.

"So, you know about the Sons of Liberty and taxes. Who has spoken to you about this?" Hill questioned.

Overcome with fear and dread, Sarah's lip started to quiver.

"Answer Mr. Hill at once, child!"

"Hush, Bridget." Hill moved even closer to Sarah. "It is best that you tell me who is responsible for speaking openly of such matters concerning the activities of this settlement, missy."

Sarah grabbed the back of the chair. "Mrs. Campbell."

"And where might I find this Mrs. Campbell?" Hill took a few steps toward Sarah.

"She's my teacher at s-s-school, I told you, and I'm not f-f-from—"

"All right, as you wish it. Your insolence and behavior have earned you an afternoon in the lockup."

"Mr. Hill, the girl is addled, surely you—"

"Enough, Bridget!" Mr. Hill held up his hand to her. "Perhaps by evening, she will be more inclined to speak when spoken to." Hill lunged at Sarah. "Umph!" he grunted, as she jammed the chair into his midsection.

"Stay away from me!"

"Why you..." Hill leaped forward, grabbed her left arm and shoved her toward a back room. "Servants don't give the orders around here!"

Anna gasped and covered her mouth. "Oh, no! Grandmother, do something!"

"Hold your tongue, Anna," Grandmother said.

"Ow! Let me go!" But the harder Sarah struggled, the tighter Hill gripped. Like a wildcat, she raked her fingernails across his face. Blood trickled down his cheeks.

The clerk slapped her across her face and sent her reeling across the stone floor. Anna started sniffling.

"Stay away from me, you monster!" Sarah staggered, regained her footing, and darted for the door.

Hill dashed after her. He grabbed his club off the wall and swung it hard. Sarah ducked and the clerk twisted and stumbled. "Oof!" When he righted himself, he grabbed her collar and ripped the neckline of her blouse, sending the tiny whalebone buttons bouncing across the floor. With his large, powerful hands, he grabbed her hair and pinched her ear. She dropped to the floor.

"Ow! Help me, Mrs. Ruggles!"

The old woman moved away, and Anna whimpered. "Grandmother, make him stop!" Mrs. Ruggles turned Anna's face away. Anna sobbed, and her shoulders shook. She held tight to her grandmother's cloak.

Crack! Smack! "Aaah! Get your hands off me!"

Hill wedged his club under Sarah's armpit and wrestled her through the doorway toward the iron bars. He retrieved his keys. Sarah head-butted the clerk, kicked him in the shins and bit his thick wrist.

Whack! The clerk brought his heavy club down across her back. While Sarah hunched over and covered her head, Hill stuck his key in the lock and opened the iron bars. With a thud, he catapulted her into the jail cell.

"Perhaps an afternoon is not severe enough! A *full* night in a cold cell will no doubt cool you down!" Hill struggled to draw the heavy bars closed. Clank! The tiny cell shook.

"Nooo!" Sarah moaned as she watched Hill test the door. She scrambled to her feet and grabbed the black iron bars. "Let me out of here!"

"You're not going anywhere, you animal!" The clerk, red-faced and panting, drew in a long breath, cleared his throat and stalked off.

Sarah jumped to her feet. "Mrs. Ruggles! Anna! Why are you just standing there? Get me out of here!" Sarah watched with pleading eyes as a frantic Mrs. Ruggles ushered Anna out the door. Sarah dropped onto the cell floor. She wept and wept until she could weep no more. Badly bruised and her spirit broken, she fell asleep.

CHAPTER 5

When Sarah awoke, it was still daylight. Her head pounded and her shoulders ached. She rolled up her sleeves and lifted her dress to check out her bruises. She ran her hand across her tender face, limped toward the window, and wondered how long she had been sleeping. With no clock in sight, she wished for her sports watch.

Standing on her tiptoes, Sarah peered out her cell window into the town square. The villagers were going about their daily routines. Across the lane, a blacksmith pumped a bellows and banged an iron mallet to shape a red-hot horseshoe. A horse-drawn cart, loaded with fruits and vegetables, plodded down the street. Two women stood in the middle of the road gossiping, while some boys played marbles in an alleyway.

Sarah rubbed her sore back, shivered and glanced around the tiny jail cell. The walls were damp and moldy. A large spider dangled from the ceiling, while mouse droppings lined the perimeter of the floor. In the corner sat a stained chamber pot that emitted a foul odor. A thin, tin plate and spoon sat atop a stained brown and white mildew-laced quilt that smelled like sweaty gym socks.

Yuck! How will I survive a night in this miserable place? The problem with Dredge was bad enough, but now this! All I did was say that I read. I should have the right to say that. What a mess! Sarah thought, shaking her head.

"Sarah Osborne?" It was Anna. Sarah glared at her.

"Oh! Sarah, your face…does it hurt?"

"What do you think?"

Anna's face reddened, and her lips quivered. "I am so sorry this has happened to you, Sarah. I can't stop thinking about your beating. I wish I could have shown some courage and pleaded with Mr. Hill on your behalf, but I fear I am a mouse when it comes to such things. Can you forgive me?"

Sarah stared into Anna's sorrowful eyes. "Yeah, well Mr. Hill *is* a scary guy."

"Yes, he is," Anna whispered. "Sarah, I have brought you a meal." Anna passed a small bowl and a large chunk of homemade bread between two of the iron bars. Anna cringed as she watched Sarah limp over, take the food, and place it on the floor. She slid her hand under her cloak. After a quick glance over her shoulder, she whipped out Miss Prickle.

Sarah grabbed the doll and turned her back on Anna. She raised the doll up and looked her in the eyes. "Oh, Miss Prickle, I thought I had lost you." Sarah's eyes filled with tears and she slipped the doll under the waistband of her apron.

"Grandmother has asked me to prepare a chamber for you in the attic. It will truly be quite pleasant. You shall even have your own cot, much better than this gloomy place."

Sarah turned around and looked into Anna's soft, emerald eyes that were wet with tears.

The young girl brushed the tears from her eyes. "It is unfortunate that you do not understand our settlement and way of life. It is so troubling. Sarah Osborne. Weren't there rules where you came from?"

Sarah shrugged. *How can I tell her that, where I come from, we had rights?*

"You have certainly come from a place that is nothing like Guilford, or you would know how to act and hold your tongue. Where have you come from?"

Sarah looked down. *How can I tell her it's not about where I came from, it's about when!* Sarah sighed. "If I told you…you wouldn't…you're right! I'll begin right now," Sarah said, folding her arms across her chest.

Anna narrowed her eyes and stared at Sarah. "What will you begin, Sarah Osborne?"

"Holding my tongue."

"Hurry along in there!" Mr. Hill bellowed. Sarah's body stiffened.

"When you come home we shall talk more," Anna whispered.

Sarah pursed her lips. *No way, sister! I'm not saying anything to anyone*! Sarah thought, as Anna scurried out the door.

The aroma of beef stew wafted through the cell and reminded Sarah of her mother's delicious food. Sarah smiled as she remembered watching her mother cook, while they both munched on celery and carrot sticks and chatted about school and girlfriends. A wave of homesickness coursed through her, but she knew it was pointless to sulk. The sound of footsteps and a man's voice interrupted Sarah's thoughts.

"Good day, Nathaniel."

"Good day, Thaddeus. What can I do for you?" Sarah stood sideways and cocked her left ear toward the sound of the voices.

"I need a strong yoke for my oxen. Mine has broken beyond repair. I wish to find a trade for my Brown Bess.

She is in very good condition. I would even throw in the gunpowder horn if necessary. I cannot get much planting done without the oxen."

"Does she shoot straight?" Mr. Hill asked.

"If the person aiming her does," Thaddeus and Hill chuckled.

"Well, I'll wager someone will be interested in this beauty," Hill said. "She's a fine-looking musket. Kindly post your name and your need, Thaddeus, and I will keep the gun here so that anyone interested will be able to inspect her."

There was a pause while Thaddeus wrote.

"That should do it," Hill said. "Now tell me, will you be attending the meeting in New Haven on the 23rd?"

"Not I! I'll not associate with the likes of the Sons of Liberty. They are nothing but rabble-rousers!"

The Sons of Liberty? Sarah gripped the bars and pressed her ear against them.

"Thaddeus, the colonies are hardly back on their feet after that dreadful war with France, and then Parliament prohibits our trade with the West Indies. We are forced to trade with England and taxed on those goods. And now King George requires stamps on all our documents. Newspapers? Wills? Marriage licenses? What will he tax next? Fig pudding?"

Whoa! This is about The Stamp Act, right out of the social studies book! Sarah thought.

"Remember, Nathaniel, England waged war to secure land for our colonies. Wars are costly, I daresay! King George needs to pay for his expense. If he cannot rely on his colonies, then—?"

"Is it not enough that some of our brothers, sons, fathers, cousins, and friends have paid with their lives, while some of us go on grieving and live with our own wounds of war? Is that not good enough for His Royal Highness?"

"Nathaniel, I will not argue that dealing with England continues to be costly, but we owe allegiance to the Motherland. Once the debt is paid, I am sure King George will let us be."

"Of that, we cannot be certain, unless we speak out against this now, it may only get worse! Surely, Thaddeus, you favor our demand for representation in Parliament?"

"Nathaniel, I share your displeasure with Parliament, taxes, and our lack of representation, but I will not talk treason, nor shall *I* become involved with the Sons of Liberty—traitors, all of them. I am a loyal subject of the Crown, and the law is the law. Tread softly and consider the consequences for you and your family should you turn against the King. Think of your dear Penelope and your children were they to have to bear the disgrace of your treason. The threat of a hangman's noose is not something to be taken lightly."

"Hmph. Well then, may I trust you will never speak of this conversation?"

Sarah snorted. "Well, Miss Prickle, it seems that Mr. Hill needs to learn when to hold his tongue, too."

"Nathaniel, the conversation is safe with me. I do not wish to be involved in any way. In any event, I will not be attending the meeting. No good will come of it. I will stop by in a few days to see if there is any interest in the musket. Thank you, and a good day to you."

Mr. Hill better hope his friend doesn't say anything, Sarah thought. She bent over to check the bruises on her shins and arms and picked up Miss Prickle. "It makes sense, though," she whispered. "If it's really April 1765, then the Stamp Tax is the law. Whoa! These people don't know they'll soon be in a War for Independence!" Sarah propped herself against the wall and slid her sore body down to the floor. She then seated Miss Prickle next to her.

Some colonists want to remain loyal to the king and their Mother Country because that's what they feel is right, and others want the colonies to be a brand-new country with no British laws. Both sides want representatives in Parliament. I wonder why King George won't let them? My dad used to complain about paying taxes, but at least he got to vote. Why shouldn't the colonists? If the colonists didn't fight so hard, we'd probably still be under British rule. Maybe I would have grown up as an English citizen. Instead, I'm an

All-American girl with state senators to represent me. Sarah thought. "Wow! This isn't a school play, Miss Prickle; it's the real thing!"

Sarah's stomach let out a long, low growl. She uncovered the warm bowl of pottage. The hearty beef aroma filled the air and brought a smile to her face. She dipped the crusty bread into the stew. Eating slowly, she savored every bite. She propped up Miss Prickle in front of her. "Want some?" She placed a spoonful of stew in front of the doll's face. "Better eat up. Don't wait for Mr. Hill to give you anything; it'll have cooties."

"No! Ow!" somebody yelled from the front office. Sarah heard feet scuffling and two loud thuds.

"Nathaniel, I pray you'll throw this young whippersnapper into the lockup. He has been riding the cows and chasing the grazing sheep. I warned him a week ago. I cannot permit abuse of the animals."

Sarah tensed up. *Not Dredge again,* she thought.

Dredge charged around the corner, holding fast to a squirming teenager. Hill followed.

"In he goes, Jacob."

"B-B-But Mr. Dredge, the tinsmith will thrash me if I don't return!"

"And *I'll* thrash you if you don't get into that cell! Now move!" Dredge grabbed the teen by the collar and shoved his face against the bars while Hill whipped out his keys.

"Umph!" the boy grunted.

Sarah drew up her knees and watched as the young man struggled to get loose. She remembered Dredge's vise-like grip. *You're not going anywhere,* she thought.

Dredge stopped short when he spotted Sarah. "It's *you* again?" he growled.

Sarah tightened her jaw and glared at the watchman.

"Ah, the good Reverend had his fill of you and turned you out."

Sarah folded her arms across her chest and then turned her back to the watchman.

"I see your manners have not improved."

"Jacob, you did not give me a chance to warn you that our lockup already has an occupant." Hill inserted a key into the keyhole.

"Well, missy, you have company." Dredge yanked the cell door open and shoved the boy in.

The boy skidded across the floor and landed with a thud.

Dredge closed the cell door and locked it. "Nathaniel, I am off to report to our tinsmith that he shall not have the use of his apprentice for two days. Perhaps a couple of days in the lockup will teach this young man not to annoy the animals." Dredge tipped his hat, threw his shoulders back and strode off.

CHAPTER 6

Sarah stared at the tall, thin teen. His messy blond hair fell across a pair of blue jay-colored eyes, and his white shirt and collar, like her white cap, sported Dredge's black, smudged fingerprints. A pair of leather suspenders held up his gray breeches. He wore white knee socks and black buckled shoes.

"Who are *you*?" he asked, staring at the bruises on Sarah's face.

"Sarah." She looked away.

"What did you do?"

Sarah frowned. "Who's asking?"

"Will Bayers. Most people around here know me. I am serving an apprenticeship with Mr. Larson, the town tinsmith." He straightened and threw back his shoulders. "So, what did you do that Mr. Hill put you in here?"

"I have nothing to say about that!" Sarah said, shaking her head.

"Well, you seemed to have gotten more than just a thrashing. How old are you?" Will asked, looking at Sarah's swollen ear.

"Eleven. How old are you?"

"Fourteen. Why can't you tell me about it?"

She shrugged her sore shoulders. "It's a long story."

"My hunch is that we will both have the time to tell our long stories." He smiled.

Sarah squelched a laugh and then looked at the floor. "I don't want to talk about it, but . . . *you* could talk about what *you* did."

Will cocked his eyebrow and scooched down next to Sarah. "Well then, I was returning to the shop after delivering a lantern to Goodwife Stone when Mr. Dredge spotted me taking a ride on the back of one of the grazing cows." Will lowered his head.

"And?" Sarah said.

"And he brought me here."

"That's it?" Sarah said.

Will nodded.

"Look, if you don't want to tell me the whole story, I understand," Sarah said.

"I have told you everything."

"No, you didn't."

"What more can I say? I did that, and now I am being punished."

"Whose cow was it?"

"Farmer Chadwick's."

"When you did that, did anyone get hurt?" Sarah asked.

"No."

"Were you *stealing* the cow?" Sarah asked gingerly.

"No."

"Did somebody *think* you were stealing it?"

"No, not at all."

"Then why did Dredge toss you in jail?"

"I have not heeded his warnings."

"But isn't jail too much of a punishment for joyriding a cow?"

"I believe so, but that's our Mr. Dredge."

"Do you have a horse?" Sarah asked.

"No."

"Then, next time you get the urge, you may want to pay someone to ride his horse."

"Well, I will certainly consider that." He chuckled. "Sarah, if you can't tell me what you did, at least tell me why your beating was so severe."

"Because the more I fought back, the madder he got," Sarah said.

"What do you mean, fought back?"

"You know, I kicked and punched him, I even bit his wrist." Will stared at her.

"My, such boldness and brazenness! Simply unheard of! Nobody fights back, much less a young Negress. Sarah, your offense is most serious," Will said.

"Wait a minute; we were talking about you. Look at the bright side, when you leave, you'll go back to where you belong, and this mess will be over for you. It's not the same for me. In a way, you're lucky," Sarah said.

"I am far from lucky. When I am returned to Mr. Larson, I'm sure he will remind me with a thrashing that he won't keep an apprentice who participates in tomfoolery."

"What's an apprentice?"

"One who learns a trade under a master craftsman." The boy looked Sarah over. "From your manner of speech and your unusual ideas, I'll wager you're a runaway, Sarah. No doubt, you'll have your time at the whipping post as well when your master claims you."

Sarah cringed and stifled her urge to tell her story. She picked up the bowl and bread. She felt Will's eyes on her as she scooped up a mouthful of the pottage. "Want some?" She raised a spoonful toward Will.

Will's eyebrows shot up. "Why, it would be improper."

"Well, I wouldn't count on Mr. Hill giving you much." Sarah lifted the stew to her lips.

"Wait, why would it be improper?"

"Because you are a Negress, of course."

Sarah scowled at Will and drew out a healthy spoonful of stew. She held it up for Will to see it and smell it, and then popped it into her mouth. "Yum," she said, smacking her lips. "This tastes sooo good. Mrs. Ruggles sure makes delicious pottage."

Will stared at her lips.

"Mm. Too bad you don't want some. Oh, that's right; you don't want to be improper. You're probably saving your appetite for what Mr. Hill will serve you later, or maybe Mr. Dredge went home to cook your dinner." Sarah bent over, held her ribs and chuckled.

"Well, perhaps I should not be so particular." He reached into his pocket and pulled out a tin spoon. Sarah held onto her ribcage and giggled.

"Wow, you're prepared! Are you a boy scout?" Sarah tore off a hunk of bread, dipped it in the stew and offered it to Will. He folded it and shoved it in his mouth and then dipped his spoon into the bowl for more.

"This is delicious," Will said.

"Anna Ruggles brought it to me."

"I know her. Her grandfather is our minister," he said.

In a matter of moments, the stew disappeared. "I am grateful for your generosity, Sarah."

She smiled as Will mopped up the sides of the bowl with the last morsel of bread.

"There, perfectly clean." He held up the bowl.

Sarah took the bowl and limped over to place it next to the quilt. "Oooh," she said, running her hands over her neck and shoulders.

"Your eye is rather swollen. Mr. Hill's handiwork, no doubt," Will said.

Sarah nodded and stroked her right eye. "He hit me right here with his thick stick."

Will shook his head. "His beatings are hard to forget."

"Yes."

Sarah, grateful for Will's company, listened as he spoke of his family. She learned that they lived on a nearby farm and that he had two older brothers, Joshua and Matthew.

"Mother runs the farm. Father is a shipwright. He loves building and repairing ships and being close to all the activity in the harbor." Will sat up straight and puffed out his chest. "I was the first of my family to apprentice in the village. My father permitted it because Mr. Larson agreed to release me during planting and harvest time. In seven days, I'll join my family in the fields. If two of those days are to be spent in the lockup, Mr. Larson will take it out on my hide."

"He'll beat you?"

Will let go a deep sigh. "He is certain to, but generally my master is fair with me. My parents have contracted with him that I will be indentured until I am twenty-one."

"What does that mean?"

"He keeps me fed, gives me a new set of clothing every year, and teaches me to read, write, and do my figures. In exchange, for the next seven years, I assist him in his shop and work by his side learning the trade." Will jumped to his feet and threw back his shoulders. "And someday, Sarah, I will have my own tin shop. I will be Will Bayer's, Village Tinsmith, at your service." He bowed deeply.

Sarah grinned. "Are your friends apprentices, too?"

"Yes. Unfortunately, some have impatient masters who beat them as if they were slaves. Some have run away, so I don't know where they are."

Sarah swallowed hard and hung her head.

Will frowned and kneeled down next to Sarah. "Why do you ask me so many questions? Are you concerned about your own punishment? What did you do?"

Sarah sighed. "Well, you see . . . I. . .fell and hit my head and Mr. Dredge found me in the village. So, he dragged me to the parsonage, and I spent the night there. Mrs. Ruggles brought me over here this morning and Mr. Hill and I argued, and well, I'm here for the night."

"*No one* in the village, let alone a servant, *dares* to disagree with Mr. Hill! He is quite quick-tempered, as you no doubt noticed." Will shook his head. "Your actions and your speech tell me you are not from around here. Where are you from?"

"Well, I hit my head. Now I'm addled and can't remember." Sarah looked away.

"Oh, I see, "Will said.

"Are there any other Negroes in Guilford?" Sarah asked.

Will sat down again. "There is a family that works in the fields on the Johnson farm just outside of town, and of course, Moses at the shipyard. You would like Moses, he speaks to everyone. Whenever I visit Father, he tells me brilliant seafaring tales of long ago and teaches me old sailing songs."

Sarah leaned closer to Will. "Teach me one?"

Will placed his finger under his chin and gave Sarah a mischievous look. "Alright, I'll give it a go." He smiled.

Ooh, what do you do with a drunken sailor?
What do you do with a drunken sailor?
What do you do with a drunken sailor earlye in the mornin'?

Shave his belly with a rusty razor!
Shave his belly with a rusty razor!
Shave his belly with a rusty razor earlye in the mornin'!

Way hay and up she rises
Way hay and up she rises
Way hay and up she rises
Earlye in the mornin'!

Sarah squealed with delight. "More, Will, more!"

Ooh, what do you do with a drunken sailor?
What do you do with a drunken sailor?
What do you do with a drunken sailor earlye in the mornin'?

Sarah clapped her hands to the rhythm.

Swab the decks with his beard and mustache!
Swab the decks with his beard and mustache!
Swab the decks with his beard and mustache earlye in the morning!
Way hay and up she rises
Way hay and up she rises
Way hay and up she rises earlye in the mornin'!

"Sing more, Will!"

"I should not. The other verses are not proper for your ears." Will leaned in and lowered his voice. "Now about Negroes and how they are treated, many of the villagers disagree with slavery, and the Negroes in this vicinity are treated fairly as long as they know their place. Cruelty is rarely seen."

I guess I'm a rare case. Sarah thought.

"Why, if my parents knew I shared a meal with *you*, both of us would get a trouncing."

Sarah grimaced.

"So, sharing the pottage will be our little secret." Will winked. He licked his spoon and placed it back in his pocket. "It's best to hold your tongue in Guilford, Sarah, and don't lock horns with Mr. Hill."

All this hold-your-tongue business! So, THIS is how it was before the Constitution gave us freedom of speech? Sarah thought.

"Well, let's stop talking of such unpleasantness." Will slipped his hand into his pocket and drew out a long piece of twine. Threaded in the center of the twine was a large brown button. He grabbed both ends of the twine and twirled the twine around in front of him like a miniature jump rope. Then he pulled the twine, and the button buzzed and danced back and forth along the twine. Sarah grinned and leaned in to watch.

"What is it called?"

"A whirligig."

"It's just a button and a string! Pretty ingenious!" Sarah stared at the contraption.

"Yes. Would you like to try it?" Will said.

"Sure." Sarah took the toy and twirled and pulled. The button slid back and forth and made a buzzing sound just as it had for Will. "It's so simple to make and so much fun! I love it!" She handed it back to Will.

A blast of cool air whooshed through the cell. "Nathaniel, I have come to speak with the girl." Reverend Ruggles rounded the corner. When the parson saw Will, he stopped short. "When did *he* arrive?" Will sprang to his feet, pocketed the whirligig and moved to the farthest corner away from Sarah.

"Dredge brought him in an hour ago," Hill replied.

"My, our Mr. Dredge has been quite busy. How long is the boy to stay?" the Reverend asked.

"Two days."

Reverend Ruggles peered over his eyeglasses. "Nathaniel, it is improper for the two of them to spend the night together. I must insist that you release the girl to me and I will deal with her firmly."

Mr. Hill glared at Sarah. "The girl is nothing but a dishonest runaway, Reverend. She is brazen and lacks respect. She needs a lesson from the strong arm of the law, not the coddling you offer at the parsonage. Frankly, I am surprised that you would want her behavior to go unpunished."

"The girl hit her head and is addled, my good sir. It was her treatment at Mr. Dredge's hands that caused the problem! At the parsonage, the girl acted most properly!"

Will and Sarah exchanged quick glances.

"I doubt that, sir!" Mr. Hill said, crossing his arms across his chest.

"Nathaniel, she is a stranger to this settlement. Surely you have heard the Good Book's advice to love the stranger? When you are kind to the stranger, you do God's work."

Hill's eyes bulged as he shook his finger at the preacher. "Your Good Book also states that a person is punishable for his actions. This girl does not know her place or when to speak."

The Reverend nodded his head. "True, she does have a problem controlling her tongue." He pointed to Hill." But if *you* keep the two of them locked up together this evening, *you* will need to contend with every tongue in the village!"

Way to go, Reverend Ruggles! Sarah thought.

Mr. Hill glared at Sarah. The base of his thick neck reddened and Sarah watched as the flush spread across his cheeks. Suddenly, his tight lips formed a strange sneer. "You are most correct, Reverend. The village *will* be gossiping by the morning. They would think I had taken leave of my senses. Slowly and deliberately he drew his keys from his pocket and approached the iron bars.

Reverend Ruggles smiled and stood with hands folded at his waist while Hill opened the cell door. Clang! Click!

Finally, I'm getting out of this dump! Sarah thought.

"Make haste, boy!" Mr. Hill looked at Will. "Explain to Mr. Larson why you were detained. He'll deal with you properly."

Will straightened up. He looked at the faces of the two men as he passed through the open cell door, cast a look of sympathy toward Sarah, and quickly bounded out. Clank. The clerk secured the door once again.

"Yes," sneered Hill. "What *would* the village say, Reverend, if they thought I had released the unknown Negro girl instead of Will Bayers?"

Clenching his jaw, the preacher stared at the clerk.

Sarah sprang to her feet searching the faces of the two men. She pressed her face against the bars. Her lower lip quivered. "Reverend Ruggles?" she whimpered through a blur of tears.

The Reverend looked into Sarah's pleading brown eyes and then turned to Hill. Through clenched teeth, he spoke, "I will be by to get the girl first thing on the morrow."

Hill smirked at Sarah.

Sarah gripped the iron bars. "No! Reverend Ruggles! Don't leave me here!" she cried.

The preacher turned away. With head down and his shoulders sagging, he departed.

CHAPTER 7

Sarah gazed through the cell window, as Miss Prickle lay on the floor next to the bowl. She drifted over to the doll and winced as she bent down to pick her up. Sarah's shoulders, back, and arms throbbed. She held the doll in front of her and looked into her tiny eyes. "Miss Prickle, what will we do?" She whispered.

Sarah sat, placed Miss Prickle on her lap, and listened as Mr. Hill transacted his daily business with villagers. The milliner came by to drop off a hat that Hill's wife had ordered.

"Good day, Nathaniel."

"Cordelia, nice to see you."

"Nathaniel, I have Penelope's bonnet, and I am extremely excited to hear what she will say about it. Your dear wife was quite patient to wait for the ostrich feathers to be shipped. The plumes are exquisite! I simply must show you."

"Cordelia, that won't be necessary. I am sure it is of the utmost quality. You needn't remove it from the box."

"Nonsense! After all, Nathaniel, I daresay it is your pocket that is paying a pretty penny for it! Penelope told me not to be stingy with materials, and I certainly was not. I simply must model it for you."

Sarah heard a rustle of paper.

"There. Is it not the loveliest bonnet you have ever seen, Nathaniel? Am I not the best milliner in the settlement? And you must tell Penelope that I used my finest silk ribbon to create that—."

"Ah...ah choo! I...ah...ah choo!"

"Good gracious! Are you ill, Nathaniel?"

"Get those bloody feathers out of my ...ah choo... office, Cordelia!"

"Why, I never! Those are *not* feathers; they are imported *plumes* of the highest quality! I expect I must deliver the bonnet directly to Penelope, now. I am certain she will—"

"Ah-choo! Get out of my office, now!" Hill roared. "And I forbid you to bring that bonnet near my house.

Turkey and quail feathers have always adorned my wife's hats before, and they will continue to suffice."

"Nathaniel Hill, you are rude and unappreciative, and for the likes of me, I cannot understand how dear, sweet Penelope, or anyone else in this settlement, can endure your ill humor!" Bang! The milliner slammed the door on her way out.

"Women!" Hill growled.

A man came by to post a letter telling of his uncle's death. "I worry that my family in England will not hear the news," he said.

"I can assure you, Josiah, they will have the news by September and my condolences to your mother on the loss of her brother. Clarence will be missed by townspeople who frequent the tavern. He was a sublime teller of tales. May he rest in peace." Hill said.

"Thank you, Nathaniel. I will relay your sentiments to mother. She is keeping herself occupied baking death cakes for the funeral; while I must order a pine box from the cabinetmaker for the burial. Good day."

Sometime in the afternoon, Mr. Tilson, the glass-blower, dropped off a bottle filled with rosewater to freshen Hill's office.

Yeah, I'm not the only one who thinks Mr. Hill stinks, Sarah thought.

But to most of his visitors, Hill delivered one corny sales pitch after another in hopes of selling Thaddeus' musket.

"Miss Prickle, it's a good thing computers haven't been invented yet. Can you imagine Mr. Hill on a computer? He would smash it with his club because it would know more than he does." She sighed. "This world is so different from the one I'm used to; people are mean. I guess it's not different for you though; this is where you came from!"

As the afternoon wore on, the blacksmith stopped by to place a posting for a new apprentice, the cooper finished a barrel and wanted to post a trade for some chickens, and the cobbler stopped by to fit Mr. Hill for a pair of boots and listen to him complain about his wife's new hat.

At the last glimmer of sunlight, Mr. Hill whipped around the corner and passed a glass of water between the iron bars. "Judging from the generous portion of pottage you had earlier, you won't need anything until morning. Make use of the little light you have left to roll out your bedding."

As Sarah touched the quilt, a large, hairy spider crept out from between the folds. She stomped on it and stifled a squeal.

"Now that's a good girl." Hill smiled. "You will find that obedience and silence will serve you well."

Sarah looked at the floor and hoped that Hill would go away so she wouldn't be forced to lie down on the dirty bedroll. When she looked up, he glowered at her and then left. She dreaded spending another night on a hard floor.

After Sarah used the chamber pot, she covered it with the end of the smelly bedroll. She picked up the cup of water, sniffed it, took a sip and rolled it around on her tongue. Detecting nothing unusual, she gulped it down. Untying her coif, she folded it into a miniature-size pillow for her head. She unbuttoned her cloak, spread it out on the dirt floor, and curled up inside it with Miss Prickle. The faint scent of lavender tissue paper still lingered on the doll.

Sarah wondered if Mr. Larson had thrashed Will and whether Will was thinking about her. She prayed that *somebody* was thinking about her and that her entire neighborhood was searching for her. Maybe the police had issued an Amber Alert.

But how can I be here if I haven't even been born? It doesn't make sense. Nothing makes sense, she thought. With confusion and uncertainty racing through her mind, Sarah drifted into a deep, sound sleep.

When the light of dawn streaked through her cell window, Sarah awoke. "Ooh," she moaned as she held her sides and limped to the chamber pot. She neatened up the bedroll, stacked the dishes, smoothed her hair, and prayed that Reverend Ruggles would come shortly.

Although her body ached, Sarah knew she needed to work her muscles. "Stretch every morning to keep those muscles limber," Coach Farrell used to say.

Launching into fifty pogo jumps, Sarah pretended she was surrounded by her teammates. She didn't stop until she had done all of them. After she completed thirty seal jacks to work her shoulders, she clasped her hands behind her head and lowered herself to the floor. Twenty prisoner squats stretched her hamstrings. She was finishing up her Spiderman lunges when she heard Mr. Hill lumber into the office.

The cool morning air, laden with the crisp scent of dew and evergreens, whooshed into her cell. Sarah took a deep breath and smiled. *I never knew that air could smell so delicious.*

"Awake, are you?" Hill stood in front of the iron bars and surveyed the cell. "Where did you get *that*?" He pointed to Miss Prickle.

"From Anna Ruggles."

"Good girl, your night in lockup has taught you obedience. I asked a question, and you answered it." He beamed. "It appears you have had ample time to ponder your brash behavior."

Sarah turned towards the window.

"Ah, not too talkative this morning? Well, perhaps it's for the best." Sarah heard the front door open.

"Is anyone here?" Reverend Ruggles called out.

Sarah smiled. The cool, fragrant air washed over her once again.

"I have come for the girl, Nathaniel."

Sarah donned her coif and cloak and gathered up Miss Prickle and the dishes. She rushed to the iron bars.

"Not so fast," Hill said.

Sarah and Reverend Ruggles froze. Their eyes met.

"Surely you don't think *I* am to clean your dirty chamber pot. There is a storage barrel in the back. Pour your waste in there and don't get any foolish notion of running away, or I will find you, and it will be unpleasant." The clerk turned the key and dragged open the cell door.

Sarah handed the dishes and Miss Prickle to the preacher. She lifted the pot and plodded out the door and around the building. When she came to the worn wooden barrel, she raised the chamber pot and splattered the contents over Mr. Hill's back steps.

"Oops! How careless of me!" Sarah grinned. She hustled back and placed the chamber pot on the cell floor. Reverend Ruggles handed Miss Prickle to her.

As they started to leave, Hill blocked their path. "Before you leave, girl, I must caution you that I shall search for your rightful owner, and I have posted your description.

When your owner comes forward, I will report to him concerning your brazenness."

Sarah's brown eyes met Hill's steel gray ones. "I hope you *do* find my *rightful* owner, Mr. Hill."

"Good day, Nathaniel, I will see you at service on the Sabbath." The Reverend peered into the clerk's eyes. "You will greatly benefit from my sermon."

CHAPTER 8

When Sarah and Reverend Ruggles returned to the parsonage, Grandmother and Anna were preparing breakfast. The preacher nodded to his wife and hurried to the barn.

Mrs. Ruggles gently clasped Sarah's shoulders and turned her to inspect the bruises on her swollen face. "Gracious, child." She shook her head.

Anna moved close to Sarah. "You look so sad. Was it awful? Did you sleep? I prayed you could sleep!"

"Anna, fetch her a cool wet cloth for her face and stop your fussing!" Mrs. Ruggles said. Anna hurried off.

"Sit, child. No doubt, your injuries cover your entire body. It is a blessing that you are young and strong, you will heal quickly." Sarah glared at her.

Anna handed her a damp rag and Sarah patted her cheeks, lips, and forehead. "Does it hurt?" Anna asked.

Sarah narrowed her eyes at Mrs. Ruggles. "Yes, but I am strong and will heal quickly." She handed back the washrag.

Anna smiled. "You *are* strong, Sarah." Sarah half-smiled as her eyes filled with tears.

Reverend Ruggles sauntered into the kitchen, and Anna and Grandmother laid out the morning meal. When everyone had settled at the table, they bowed their heads, and the minister said the blessing.

"Most Heavenly Father, thank you for your bountiful gifts. We ask that you look kindly upon this family and guide Sarah in tempering her speech. We pray you to instill Mr. Hill and Mr. Dredge with a true sense of justice and compassion as they fulfill their duties in our settlement. Amen."

"Amen," the women answered.

Sarah scarfed down two cornmeal biscuits dripping with honey, two large goose eggs, a piece of browned beef and a cup of warm milk.

"Anna, please collect the eating utensils and trenchers and fill the sink." Mrs. Ruggles said as the Reverend left to finish the milking. "Sarah, go into the study. I must speak with you."

Sarah limped toward the study.

"Why are you walking that way?" Mrs. Ruggles asked.

Sarah lifted her skirt and stuck out her left leg.

"My word!" Mrs. Ruggles gasped as she viewed the purple, splotchy bruises that ran from Sarah's ankle to her thigh.

Sarah lowered her skirt and sat down in front of the fireplace.

"No doubt it was a rather unpleasant experience. The Reverend and I believe that Mr. Hill was too firm with you and the whole incident was regrettable. Now that you are back in this house, you will be in our employ until further notice, and I must warn you to hold your tongue. Boldness will not be tolerated. You will do as you are told and perform your duties in a timely fashion. Do you understand, child?"

Sarah looked into the woman's pinched face. "Yes."

"It's yes, Mrs. Ruggles."

"Yes, Mrs. Ruggles." Sarah looked down at her hands.

"It is a blessing that the good Lord has sent you to us during planting time; there will be much to do in the garden. I daresay another pair of hands will be useful. Anna has set up a bed for you in the attic. Follow me, and I will show you. Bring your cloak and the poppet."

As Sarah climbed the stairs, she winced and placed one hand on the wall to steady herself. The attic was dark except for a little light gleaming in through one small window. After Mrs. Ruggles lit a tiny oil lamp, Sarah looked around. There were some household goods and wooden boxes stacked in the corner, and some men's clothes hung on brass hooks, secured to low wooden beams. Near the window stood a short cot, with a small pillow, and the quilt that had covered her on the first night. At the foot of the cot sat a plain wooden trunk.

"You are a bit tall, but you will find the bed more suitable than your sleeping conditions of late." Mrs. Ruggles lifted the latch to the trunk. "Place your belongings in here. I expect to see that your garments are neatly folded each evening. Since you seem to have some schooling, you will join us each evening for reflection." She fished a Bible out of the trunk and handed it to Sarah.

Sarah felt the old woman's eyes on her. "Thank you, Mrs. Ruggles."

"Very well, then. Put on your cloak and go help Anna fill the sink. After that, you will help her feed the chickens and muck the garden."

Sarah tossed Miss Prickle onto her cot and followed Mrs. Ruggles down the staircase. She proceeded into the kitchen and through the back door.

Outside, Sarah worked her way down a large stone walkway and came upon two smaller cobblestone paths. Veering left, she arrived at a large L-shaped barn with its doors wide open. As she stepped across the threshold, she smelled fresh hay mixed with the musky odor of animal sweat. Above her were thick wooden rafters piled high with neat bundles of hay, and farm tools hung on the walls. There were three stalls, a mound of hay in each.

As she walked by the high wooden stalls, Sarah noticed that the first two were empty. In the third one, a hefty ewe cuddled her three babies and gave Sarah a curious look. Sarah opened the gate and tiptoed over.

"Good morning, madam." Kneeling next to the animals, she ran her fingers through the mother's warm thick fleece. "What a beautiful family you have." The tiny lambs had cotton candy coats with wide eyes too large for their faces. "Oh, you are little bitty things, aren't you? I wonder what your names are."

"The mother's name is Abby. We haven't named the lambs yet."

Sarah jumped. "Oh, Reverend Ruggles! I'm looking for Anna."

"I do not see her in Abby's stall." He smiled. "I think you will find her bringing water up from the stream to the dry sink. If you go back and follow the other path, you are sure to find her."

Sarah nodded and took a deep breath. "Reverend Ruggles, thank you for trying to get Mr. Hill to release me."

The minister peered over his glasses at her. "You are welcome. Mrs. Ruggles relayed to me what happened, and although it was quite brazen of you, I did not think it warranted such strict discipline. Apparently, Mr. Hill thought otherwise. Sarah, there are lessons for both you and Mr. Hill to learn."

"Lessons for me? All I did was read."

Reverend Ruggles squatted, gently clasped Sarah's shoulders and looked into her face. "When Mr. Hill wielded his authority without compassion, he was wrong. It is my task as his minister to shepherd him onto the right path. And rest assured I will do that. But your challenge, Sarah, is to voice your opinion to your elders in a more respectful way and to forgive Mr. Hill."

"Forgive him? But I was only—"

"I know," the Reverend interrupted. "But you must learn to forgive."

Sarah sighed and gave the preacher a long look before heading down the path to find Anna.

CHAPTER 9

Threading her way past stubby, purple crocuses and pale, yellow daffodils, Sarah spotted Anna waddling down the path. Across her shoulders was a long board. Suspended from each end was a large tin pail, filled with water. Anna lowered the board and carefully placed the pails on the ground.

"I am pleased you are returned to us, Sarah Osborne. Was it very awful for you?"

"Yup, Mr. Hill is pretty mean, and my body still aches, but I met a cool kid named Will Bayers."

"Cool? Was it too cold in the lockup for Will?"

Sarah stared at Anna. "When someone is cool, it means that they're fun to be with."

"Oh."

"What is this?" Sarah pointed to the board.

"Silly girl, this is a yoke to help me carry things. I cannot manage a filled bucket in each of my hands; it is much too heavy. The yoke steadies the load and permits me to use my neck and shoulders."

"Let me try," Sarah said. She crouched down and placed the yoke over her neck and shoulders. When she stood up straight, the pails lifted off the ground. She wobbled towards the house.

"Did you not do this where you came from, Sarah Osborne?"

"Nope." The girls giggled when Sarah lost her balance and water sloshed over the sides of the buckets.

"It is good that you are carrying water rather than milk." Anna smiled.

"Anna, why do you call me Sarah Osborne?"

"Is it not your name?"

"Yes, but just call me Sarah."

Anna smiled. "Sarah, you are cool."

When the girls entered the kitchen, Mrs. Ruggles lifted the water and poured it into a rectangular-shaped wooden trough with a protruding sprout.

"Go muck the garden, girls. I have laid out the galoshes." Mrs. Ruggles nodded in the direction of the hearth.

"Oh, Sarah! You get to wear mother's galoshes!" Anna said. "I do not mean to offend, but your foot is much larger than mine. Someday, I'll grow taller and wear Mother's garments."

Sarah made a face at the ugly, brown, weathered footgear. *It's not even wet outside. Why are we putting these on?* Sarah wondered.

The girls pulled on the boots and dashed to the barn. As Anna searched for the tools, Sarah peeked into Abbey's stall and spied the lambs still cuddled up next to their mother. Anna stood on tiptoes, removed a hoe and a rake from their pegs and handed Sarah the rake. The girls walked to a dirt-filled side yard, encircled by a low stone wall. A mound of wet mud sat in the middle of the yard, and a foul odor wafted through the air. Both girls jumped over the wall and trudged to the mound.

"Wow! That stinks!" Sarah yelped, wrinkling her nose. "Ooh, Anna! Watch out! Don't step in it." She stretched her arm out in front of her friend.

Anna looked around. "Where shall I not step, Sarah?"

"In that pile. It's a pile of cow manure! Can't you smell it?"

"Yes. We must work it into the soil while it is still fresh and moist. Grandmother has instructed us to muck."

Sarah stood wide-eyed with her fingers pinching her nose shut. "How can you stand that smell?"

Anna stared at Sarah.

"Why are you looking at me like that? This *really* stinks!"

"Where on earth could you have come from, Sarah? I mean no offense, but—"

"You keep asking me that. You really wanna know? It's not *where* I come from; it's *when*."

Anna shook her head and sighed. "Sarah, mucking is necessary for our vegetables. Come, let us begin."

"Do you *really* expect me to stand in that giant toilet bowl?"

Anna's jaw dropped. "You wish to eat, do you not? The mucking will make our garden more fertile, and our yield will be better." Anna scowled and placed her hands on her hips. "Sarah, why do you not know the very things servants and villagers know? Were you a house servant for kings and queens? Why do you not know how to grow food? Did you not have the usual chores?"

"I've never farmed," Sarah said, removing her hand from her nose, "but now I guess I know what the boots are for."

Anna pursed her lips. "You will spread the manure, and I will work it into the soil. It will not be long before we will be able to plant. This garden will be for squash, peppers, and beans," Anna said.

Sarah swallowed and plunked the rake down into the soft, smelly pile, dragged out the manure, and spread it. Anna worked without speaking, and Sarah wondered what

Jerome was doing and what her friends would say if they knew she was knee deep in cow poop. Before long, Sarah got used to the smell and started humming the catchy sailor's tune that Will Bayers had sung.

"Your mood seems to have lifted," Anna said. Sarah smiled.

"Don't you go to school, Anna?"

"Yes, but not during planting season or harvest, Grandmother and Grandfather need me."

Sarah wiped away the beads of sweat that formed on her forehead. "Don't you get in trouble for not going all the time?"

"Schoolmaster Johnson understands, and when our harvests are good, Grandmother sends me to school with a supply of vegetables for him."

When the sun moved overhead, the girls removed their cloaks and switched jobs. As the mound of manure became flatter, Sarah's arms began to ache and small blisters formed on her fingers and palm. As she raised her hand to inspect a callus, she slipped and almost fell headfirst into the last heap of manure. She quickly grabbed the hoe and planted it in front of her while she struggled to regain her balance. "Phew, that was a close one!" Sarah breathed a sigh of relief.

When they finished their work, the girls returned the tools and headed back to the farmhouse.

"Thankfully, tomorrow is the Sabbath and no chores! And we'll have a warm bath this evening." Anna chirped.

"I need one now!" groaned Sarah, pinching her nose.

CHAPTER 10

Nobody told the roosters it was the Sabbath. They woke up the entire settlement at dawn. There were cows to milk, chickens to feed and preparations to be made before church. Mrs. Ruggles cooked breakfast while Anna and Sarah skipped down the walkway to the barn.

After Anna gave Sarah a quick lesson on milking, Sarah slid onto the stool and yanked on Sadie's udder. "Ooh. That feels gross!" Sarah scrunched up her face as milk flew in every direction.

"You must learn to aim the udder more accurately." Anna watched for a few more minutes while more mis-guided squirts of milk flew across Sarah's apron. "Allow me." Anna touched Sarah's shoulder, and Sarah surrendered the stool. "Go fill your apron pockets with corn kernels, Sarah. You will not need to search out the chickens, they will find you." Anna smiled and directed Sarah to the barrel of dried corn.

Sarah sprinkled the feed. Four hens, three chicks, and a rooster skirted across her path and gobbled up the corn as soon as it hit the barn's dusty floor. Sarah delighted in the cluck, cluck, clucking of the hens, the clumsiness of the peach fuzz chicks and the proud strut of the rooster. She watched as each animal revealed a different personality. Anna, struggling with a pail full of milk, moved past Sarah.

"Let me help." Sarah eased the bucket out of Anna's delicate hands without spilling a drop.

"Thank you. I will put some fresh straw and water in Abigail's stall. On our way to service, we will drop Sadie at the common to graze. Before long, Abigail will be back on the common with her little ones."

"Anna, with all the animals that graze on the green, how can you tell the ones that are yours?"

"Why I call their names, and they come to me, silly."

"Why don't they wander off?"

"The grazing is plentiful on the common. There is no reason for them to wander. Sometimes new lambs or calves roam, but they are returned, and they learn."

Before the girls headed back, they peeked in on Abigail and her babies. Sarah carried the milk to the house and placed it on the kitchen table. Grandmother nodded her approval. The hearty aroma of searing beef, pottage, and fresh bread floated through the air. Mrs. Ruggles handed each girl a biscuit and an apple for breakfast. "We must hurry, or we shall be late for service. Grandfather has already gone."

Grandmother quickly packed the food into two large woven baskets. *Maybe there's a picnic after church*, Sarah thought, as she bit into a warm biscuit. Moist with a healthy smear of butter, it tasted of raisins and cinnamon and reminded her of the sticky buns her mother bought at The Food Center Bakery after church on Sundays.

"Make haste, girls. Anna, go to the barn and fetch Sadie. Sarah, carry the pottage." She handed Sarah a basket containing a large bowl with a lid. "Carry it with care, child."

As Anna, Sarah, and Grandmother trudged to church, Anna tugged gently at the long rope tied around the cow's neck. The only sounds were the swishing of their skirts and an occasional word of encouragement to the cow.

At the common, Anna patted Sadie and untied the rope. "Eat well, Sadie. I shall see you this evening." She plunked down the rope at the foot of a big oak tree.

Grandmother passed by the church and entered a small, white house. White, pink, and purple hyacinths stood at attention in the front garden.

"Anna, who lives here?" Sarah whispered.

"No one. It is the Sabbath House where the congregation shares the midday meal. Grandmother has brought our offering."

"You mean everyone in church eats together before they go home?"

"No, Sarah. Everyone shares a meal here before we go back to afternoon services."

Sarah's eyes got wide. "Wait a minute! Church service isn't over in an hour?"

Anna cocked her head to one side and stared at Sarah. "No, the Sabbath is a holy day. The *entire* day is holy."

Sarah groaned. *A whole day in church? These people are crazy! If I were home, after church we'd go to Jerome's soccer game, the mall, or the movies,* she thought.

They stood in a large room with a fireplace. Three women stood behind a long table. A thin blonde one accepted the food, while the others sorted and arranged the offerings.

"Good morning, Bridget," a short plump woman said, holding an oval basket.

"Good morning, Rachel." I brought beef chutney, rabbit pottage, and brown bread."

"As always, you are most generous." Mrs. Ruggles smiled.

"And who might this Negress be?" Rachel asked, eyeing Sarah.

"This is Sarah," Mrs. Ruggles said. "She will be quartered at the parsonage. Sarah, this is Mrs. Bayers. Please make your manners."

Sarah extended her right hand. "Nice to meet you, Mrs. Bayers." Both women stared at the outstretched hand. Sarah felt her face flush. She pulled her hand back, and her eyes darted to Anna.

"Goodwife Bayers, it is so lovely to see you this Sabbath," Anna said, bending in a ladylike curtsy. Sarah followed with a wobbly one.

"Are you Will's mother?" Sarah asked.

"Why, yes, do you know my William?"

"Yes...uh, Mr. Dredge introduced us." Mrs. Bayers narrowed her eyes at Sarah.

"Sarah thinks Will is cool. That means that he is fun to be around." Anna grinned.

"We must get to the service. Come along girls," Grandmother ordered.

Anna, still grinning, delivered another deep curtsy and Sarah followed suit. The two girls scurried off.

The trio marched down the center aisle to the pew closest to the altar. Grandmother pushed open a small swinging door that had a tiny brass plate with *Ruggles* inscribed on it. She stepped back and motioned for Sarah to sit down at the other end of the polished, mahogany bench. Anna slid in next to Sarah, while Grandmother sat closest to the aisle.

Two worn hymnals were stacked in the corner closest to Sarah, and a narrow green and brown rug ran the length of the pew. Near Grandmother's feet sat a small footstool, and at her elbow was an armrest covered in a delicate needlepoint fabric.

"What's that?" whispered Sarah, pointing to a wide-mouthed brass container on the floor.

"Father's spittoon. He chewed tobacco during services. Grandmother never removed it."

"Shh!" Grandmother peered over her eyeglasses at the girls.

Sarah scanned the congregation and spotted Will, sitting with his family. Dressed for church, they all looked angelic. Will spied Sarah and shot her an impish wink. She smiled back and faced the altar just in time to see a thin, clean-shaven man sit down at the large pipe organ. He played a few chords, and everyone scooped up their hymnals and stood while Reverend Ruggles marched down the aisle, white clerical robe flapping, and the congregation broke into *Rock of Ages*. Sarah chimed in with her strong, rich voice and Grandmother smiled at her approvingly.

When the final chords of the song faded, the congregation sat down. Reverend Ruggles stood at the pulpit and launched into his sermon. "Do unto others as you would have them do unto you. My brothers and sisters, this is the way our Lord has asked us to live our lives. We need to strive to put the feelings and needs of our neighbors ahead of our own vanities. We are *all* worthwhile members of our community and deserve to be treated as such. The blacksmith shoes our horses, the cooper makes our barrels, the milliner creates beautiful hats, the town crier keeps us informed. *All* of the members of this village are important." The minister looked directly at Sarah. "Even our servants." Then he scanned the rows of faces until he found Mr. Hill. "When people in authority get caught up in their own self-importance and hurt others physically and emotionally in the name of justice, they are not following the Lord's greatest commandment, to do unto others as you would have them do unto you. My brothers and sisters, no one among us should take this lightly. The fine officials of our town must deal with people fairly and compassionately and punish them according to the severity of their crimes."

Sarah followed the preacher's gaze and spied a red-faced Mr. Hill, squirming in his seat. Her eyes met his sneer. *Serves you right, Mr. Hill,* she thought.

Reverend Ruggles spoke about a merciful God, a just God, a God who protects widows and orphans, and yes, even slaves. The Reverend glared at Hill who squirmed some more. Flustered, the clerk headed for the door. "Return to your seat, Mr. Hill, I have not yet completed my sermon!" Reverend Ruggles roared. "I thought *you* would be most interested in it. It speaks of fairness and kindness and respect for *all* of God's creatures."

All eyes rested on the red-faced Hill as he slithered back to his seat. Will and Sarah exchanged triumphant grins. Hill scowled at the preacher, folded his arms across his chest, and shrunk down in his seat.

Reverend Ruggles pointed an accusatory finger at the clerk. "As an appointed official in our community and a member of this congregation, it is your obligation to apply justice with mercy. The good people of Guilford look to you and others like you to be models of good character." He surveyed the congregation until he found Dredge, who was slumped down in his seat with his head lowered. "And Mr. Dredge, this applies to you as well. Even the least powerful in our settlement deserves compassion. We are *all* God's creatures."

The minister stretched his arms out across the congregation. "And it is the entire community's obligation to hold our officials to this standard. To turn a blind eye is morally wrong. As your minister, I must demand that this greatest of commandments be respected and observed in our settlement. Let us give thanks for all that we have and pray that henceforth we will all do unto others as we would have them do unto us. Let us all say Amen!"

"Amen!" the congregation answered.

As the preacher announced scripture meetings, tithing obligations, and upcoming baptisms, his voice grew monotonous. Sarah daydreamed about her family and wondered if she'd ever see them again. *How does Anna feel knowing that she will never see her parents again?* she thought.

Occasionally, Sarah tuned into something the preacher was saying, but after a while, her mind wandered. From the corner of her eye, she caught Anna fidgeting. *Does Anna ever have time to enjoy herself?* Sarah wondered.

Sarah snapped out of her daydreaming when she heard her name called. The entire congregation stared at her in silence, except for the man who was emptying his mouth of tobacco juice.

"Sarah Osborne?" Sarah sat up straight. "Kindly stand," came the preacher's voice. Sarah froze and stared at Reverend Ruggles.

"Please stand, Sarah. Do not keep Grandfather waiting." Anna whispered.

Sarah slowly stood. The floorboards under her feet creaked.

"Face the congregation, child." Reverend Ruggles said.

Her ears felt hot, and her hands grew clammy. She stared into the rows of solemn faces.

"So, my good people, if this young Negress belongs to anyone, or if you know the whereabouts of her quarters, kindly state it now."

Sarah's heart raced. *Oh no! Reverend Ruggles is putting me up for grabs! I can't believe this, anyone can claim me!*

Sarah gulped in air as her knees turned to jelly and she grabbed the pew to steady herself. How she wanted to speak, but she dared not, the memory of the horrible night in jail too fresh in her mind. She closed her eyes, waited, and prayed that this awful nightmare would end. Nobody uttered a word.

Finally, after what seemed an eternity, Reverend Ruggles spoke. "You may be seated."

Sarah collapsed into her seat.

"Thank you, my good people. The girl shall be kept at the parsonage until we find her rightful owner."

The service continued. The churchgoers sang hymns, prayed for the well-being of King George, offered petitions and contended with growling stomachs.

Finally, the organist played *I Sing the Mighty Power of God*, and the congregation processed to the Sabbath House. Sarah, drained and hungry, followed.

CHAPTER 11

At the Sabbath House, the men sat down at the tables, and most of the women and older children served them. When it came time to eat, Sarah was so famished she thought she would faint. Anna bowed her head in silent prayer before picking up her spoon. Sarah gulped down two bowls of pottage, a piece of Goodwife Stone's apple nut cake and a large cup of milk.

Anna finished first and waited patiently for Sarah. "Come, Sarah, I would like you to meet Clara and Prudence."

In the yard, a big, S-shaped chain of children, giggling and holding hands, sailed past Anna and Sarah. As the children in the front and middle whipped around, the boy at the end broke loose and tumbled onto the grass.

"What are they doing?" Sarah asked.

"They are playing Snap the Whip," Anna said.

Sarah grinned and watched as a few more children at the end flew off the line. "Come," Anna said, leading Sarah to two girls who were sitting and chatting under an oak tree. "Clara Stone and Prudence Johnson, I would like you to meet Sarah Osborne."

Both girls rose and curtsied. Sarah returned a perfect curtsy and Anna beamed.

"It is unfortunate that you do not know the whereabouts of your master, Sarah," Prudence said.

Sarah looked down at the ground and ran her toe across the dirt.

"We will find Sarah's rightful home someday," Anna offered. "Until then, I am fortunate to have her help me with my chores."

Prudence and Clara sat down under a tree and asked Anna and Sarah to join them. "We were just chatting about our stitchery," Prudence said. "I have run short on thread, but Mother has promised when the next ship arrives with supplies from England, she will purchase enough colorful spools and silk ribbons for me to complete my sampler. Father will construct a frame for it."

Anna clapped her hands. "Oh, Prudence! You must show it to us when it is completed!" Prudence smiled.

"And when the new gingham and muslin arrive, Mother has promised to stitch me a new Sabbath dress with a matching coif," Clara said.

"Clara, that will be dandy! I would love to persuade Grandmother to stitch a new dress for Sarah and to purchase a new pink hair ribbon for me. Perhaps she will if I am diligent in my chores."

The girls inspected Sarah's threadbare outfit. Her apron was still covered with little brown smudges and milk stains. Embarrassment crept across Sarah's face. As she looked around, only half listening to the blabbering about new clothes and stitching projects, she spied Will and his brothers scurrying around, holding sticks, and chasing a large, wooden hoop.

That's what I need, a good run, I gotta get myself moving again, even if I can't swim, Sarah thought. Homesickness washed over her when she thought of her swimming workouts at the McArthur Arena Pool.

"Oooh!" Prudence and Clara squealed as Sarah jumped up and blocked a runaway hoop that barreled toward the circle of girls.

"Can I try?" Sarah asked, holding up the hoop to the panting boy who sought to reclaim it.

The young boy stiffened and peered at Clara.

"It's fine Caleb; this is Sarah. She is with Anna."

Caleb handed Sarah the stick.

"Thanks, Caleb." Sarah grinned. She positioned the hoop like the boys had and nudged it along with the stick, but the hoop wobbled and fell over. Sarah picked it up and tried again. This time the hoop rolled and stayed upright for three strokes of the stick.

"That's better," Clara said.

"You learn quickly, Sarah!" Anna cheered.

Sarah started again and this time swatted the hoop and ran beside it as it rolled straight across the yard to where Will and his brothers were talking. The boys saw it coming toward them, and they clapped and whooped when they saw Sarah keep the hoop rolling for so long. The hoop sped straight across the yard and finally crashed at Will's feet. Sarah swooped up the hoop, lifted it over her shoulders and moved it to her waist, rotating her hips, back and forth, while the hoop whirled around her middle.

"See! A hula hoop!" she yelled with delight as she gyrated, nonstop.

"Look at Sarah!" Caleb squealed. As Anna, Prudence and Clara watched in delighted amazement, a group of smiling children surrounded Sarah and clapped in unison, keeping the beat as Sarah swayed.

As suddenly as the clapping had begun, it stopped. A hushed silence fell over the crowd of children, and the circle broke apart.

"That will be enough, Sarah."

Sarah dropped the hoop and looked up into Mrs. Ruggles's angry face. "I was just—"

"You were just displaying unladylike behavior in public, and on the Sabbath of all days! For shame, child. Take your leave now, Sarah. Return to the parsonage and go directly to your quarters."

"I wasn't doing anything wrong! I was only having fun and showing the others how to play hula-hoop. The trouble with life in this place is there's no fun, ever! I hate it here! And I hate you and your stupid rules!"

Smack! Grandmother's hand shot across Sarah's face.

Sarah gasped and stumbled. When she turned and saw looks of panic frozen on the faces of the children who moments ago had been cheering and clapping for her, she burst into tears. She sprang off across the lawn, headed for the parsonage, and didn't slow her pace until she was safely inside her attic room. She threw herself onto her cot and buried her face in the folds of Miss Prickle's dress.

"I can't stand it anymore!" Sarah screamed between sobs. "I wish I could run away, but where would I go? I want to go home! I need my family! Make it better, Miss Prickle. Please, someone, make it better." Sarah picked up the doll. "Look at what I've done to you." She smoothed out the doll's tear-stained dress and cloak and propped her up on the foot of the cot. Sarah walked over to the tiny window and peered out across the green.

As Sadie nibbled on a patch of grass, the bell in the steeple summoned the villagers back to church. At least she didn't have to return to those hard benches for the afternoon. Everyone in the village was obediently doing something, even Sarah. She had obediently come back directly to the parsonage and now was obediently waiting in her room until the rest of the obedient Ruggles returned from church. *This girl has had enough! I'm getting out of here while the getting's good,* she thought.

Sarah searched the attic and quickly found what she was looking for. In the far corner sat a large trunk, full of clothes that had belonged to Anna's father. She rummaged through it and found a pair of gray pants, a tattered white shirt, a short red vest, a pair of brown leather suspenders, and a warm black jacket with brass buttons. A blue, tri-cornered hat completed the outfit. She stripped off her apron and dress and shoved them into the trunk. *An even exchange,* she thought.

Sarah pulled on the pants and buttoned them up. She rolled the cuffs three times to make them fit and then rolled up the sleeves of the shirt. The vest didn't fit too badly, but she needed to roll up the sleeves of the jacket as well.

Twisting her braids up in a knot on top of her head, she pulled the hat down over her ears. Finally, she snatched up Miss Prickle and dropped her into the left pocket of the jacket. "Miss Prickle, we're out of here!"

As she passed by Anna's room, Sarah felt a pang of remorse for skipping out on her new young friend. She had grown to like Anna and her sweet disposition. Hurrying to the Reverend's study, she found a piece of parchment paper lying on his desk. She drew the quill pen out of the inkwell and wrote:

> Dear Anna,
> I'll miss you. Stay cool.
> Sarah

Sarah scurried back and left the note on Anna's pillow. In the kitchen, she stuffed her right jacket pocket with hard biscuits, an apple, and a dried beef stick. The clock in the study struck noon, and without looking back, Sarah fled.

CHAPTER 12

Worried that she would be pursued, Sarah hurried past the oak and elm trees that lined the main road. She hoped to find a town with understanding people who might help her go home.

When the sun was low in the western sky, she pinched off a small piece of her biscuit, collapsed onto a tree stump, and began massaging her feet. She was relieved not to be wearing that dress, apron, and cap; although after a couple of hours on the run she had considered returning to the parsonage. But, she had decided against it because the prospect of a public flogging for running away made her shudder.

The sky was heavy with thick, gray clouds and Sarah smelled the dampness of an approaching spring shower. She knew it wouldn't take long for the clouds to burst open and she would be drenched unless she found shelter. *There must be someplace to stay dry around here,* she thought. She quickened her pace when the leaves turned their backs to the wind and a thick raindrop kerplunked onto the brim of her cap. The next one hit her shoulder, and the downpour followed.

Boom! Sarah heard the roll of thunder in the distance. *Never take cover under a tree in a storm,* her mother used to say.

Up ahead, she spotted a gray blob between some branches and ran to it. *A farmhouse and barn!* She thought as the rain pelted her. She sprinted to the barn and peeked through the dusty windows. There was no one inside.

She tiptoed in and looked around. A big brown horse with a white splotch between his eyes and nose peered over the stall at her. She quietly walked his way. "Hi, big fellow." The horse issued a low whinny. "I'm not going to hurt you," she said, stroking his nose. She pulled out her apple, bit off a chunk and offered it to the horse. Scoffing it up, the horse displayed large brown and white teeth and speckled brown gums.

"I'm visiting you for a while," Sarah said as the horse licked her hand. The scratchy feel of his warm tongue against her palm tickled, and Sarah smiled. "No more for you, big guy. The rest of that apple is mine."

Sarah peeled off her wet jacket, shook it and hung it on the stall's wooden slats. She gazed out the large window and watched as rain cascaded off the roof and rolled into a beautiful pond, surrounded by a lush, green forest.

She removed her hat and shoes and wiggled her toes. After she pulled out Miss Prickle, she lay down in the straw. Looking up at the ceiling, she smiled at the sound of the rain drumming across the roof.

She held up the doll. "Hello, Miss Prickle. Did you enjoy our hike?" The doll stared back at her.

"You're kind of quiet. Are you frightened? Don't worry, I'll take care of you, and we'll get home somehow," Sarah said, snuggling the doll. To the rhythm of raindrops, Sarah drifted off to sleep.

The barn door swung open! A sudden gust of wind blew in and diluted the sweaty animal odor. The sound of heavy footsteps startled Sarah awake. She held her breath and stayed still as she peered between the wooden slats in the horse stall. *Oh no! This must be the owner,* she thought.

Just inside the barn door stood a short and stocky red-haired man. "Blessed rain! How's a gent to keep up his spirits when he's soaked from head to foot? I shall be a laughingstock if I do not dry out." His head bobbed, and his hand shook.

Without making a sound, Sarah reached up and pulled her jacket down off the stall boards and grabbed her hat. Through the slats, she watched a chunky, black puppy race through the door. He scampered around, wagging his tail.

"So, there you are," said the man. "See what happens when you leave the side of your master?" The man's voice quivered. He bent down and touched the dog's head, and the dog licked his hand. As the man removed his wet coat and snapped it in the air, a spray of raindrops landed on the dog. The dog gave a hearty shake of his fur, flinging droplets of water everywhere. "You scamp!" laughed the man, his head bobbing. "How am I to dry off with you around?" He shooed the dog away.

Sarah watched the dog scamper to the far corner of the room, leaving a trail of muddy paw prints in his wake. The man strode to the barn door watching the rain roll off the roof. As the man paced back and forth, muttering to himself, the horse let out a low whinny. The pup yelped and raced into the stall.

"Go away. Good doggie. Now go away," Sarah whispered.

The dog kept yapping.

"Culpepper! Be still!" The man called.

"Go away, Culpepper," Sarah pleaded. The dog sniffed Sarah and barked louder as the horse threw back his head and started to neigh and sidle.

"Why are you making such a fuss?"

Sarah heard the man approaching. She rolled to the corner of the cell and drew her knees to her chest. Then she shoved Miss Prickle into her pocket and pulled her cap down across her eyes. *Oh no! What am I going to do?* she thought.

"Culpepper, I..." The man stopped short. "Well, so this lad is setting you off."

Sarah stared at the stranger.

"I did not see you there, lad. I apologize if my dog frightened you or your horse." The man's head bobbed up and down when he spoke. "There, there, Culpepper. Quiet down, now."

The dog obeyed but kept a close eye on Sarah as she cautiously got to her feet and patted the horse's back. "Take it easy, fella," Sarah said.

"We just came in out of the rain," the man said. "I meant no bother."

Sarah continued to pet the horse's nose without saying a word.

"We don't mean to impose. As soon as the rain lets up, we will be on our way."

Sarah nodded.

"I do appreciate it, lad. My name is Samuel and yours might be?"

"I...I'm..." she said.

"Don't be frightened, boy. I am a harmless fellow," he said.

Sarah threw back her shoulders and smiled.

"I'm Jebediah Horatio Atkins. My friends call me Jeb."

She grinned. *Jebediah Horatio, I'll have to remember that,* Sarah thought.

"Well, young Mr. Atkins, I am pleased to make your acquaintance. I hope you will allow me to call you Jeb." Sarah nodded. Samuel and the dog left the stall and stood near the door.

Samuel removed a stick from the pocket of his tattered coat. He raised his foot and picked the mud off his boot. Sarah gave the horse one last pat across the nose and joined the man.

"Be sure to thank your master for my use of his barn." Sarah nodded once again. *Here we go again with the master thing.* Sarah stared out the door in the rain. Culpepper sniffed at her pocket. She broke off a piece of biscuit and handed it to the pup.

"You have a friend for life, lad."

Sarah chuckled. "So where are you from?"

"Boston."

Sarah gently stroked Culpepper's head. "Did you ride a horse?"

"No, horses and I don't mix, I fear. I came by coach to Saybrook, and I have already worn holes in my leather walking from there." He lifted his boot. Sarah smiled and continued stroking the pup.

"He is a Newfoundland," Samuel said, pointing to the dog.

"He'll be huge when he grows up," Sarah said.

"I daresay he will grow to be almost the size of your horse there. Your master is fortunate to have a servant boy like you. I hope he treats you fairly."

"Well, actually, I'm just passing through, too. I've been sent on an errand. When the rain lets up, I'll be on my way," Sarah said.

Samuel squinted at Sarah. "What kind of an errand?"

"I need to deliver a message to New Haven," she blurted out.

"A message is it? You don't say! And whom might the message be from?"

Sarah squirmed a bit.

"Jeb, are you a runaway?" Although Sarah's heart banged wildly, she threw back her shoulders, looked him in the eye and smiled.

"Of course, not. I'm the blacksmith apprentice for Mr. Johnson in Guilford. He cannot leave his business to attend a meeting in New Haven, so he asked me to deliver a message."

"Then you are a most trusted individual, Jeb. This meeting must be important."

"Yes, it's a meeting of the Sons of Liberty."

Samuel raised his eyebrows. "Why, I am to attend that very meeting. Perhaps I could deliver the message for you?"

"No, thank you, Samuel. I gave Mr. Johnson my word that I would deliver the message myself." Sarah blushed and stared down at her shoes.

"Well, it will soon be dark. Mr. Johnson was foolish to risk sending a young Negro out alone. If you come into the wrong company, you could be locked up until your master comes looking for you."

"It won't be the first time," she said, shuddering.

"Perhaps it would be better if you travel with me, lad. If anyone asks, you are my companion," Samuel said.

"I have a better idea. If anyone asks, you are *my* companion." She grinned.

Samuel let out a belly laugh and gave Sarah a good-natured slap across the back. "My boy, you certainly have some wit about you. I think we will make each other fine companions."

Sarah looked outside. Now that she had a protector, she wanted to get going, but the rain would not let up. *From stranger to traveling companions in a few short minutes! This is really weird. When you tell the truth, they lock you up or scold you. When you tell a whopper, they take you on as a traveling companion. Oh well, at least I can relax for a while.* She wished the rain would stop.

Samuel sat down on the dirt floor next to her. "It does not look like it is nearing an end, Jeb. We may have to wait it out until morning. At the least, we will be dry."

Sarah picked up some straw and drew crisscross lines in the dirt. "Would you like to play Tic-Tac-Toe?" she asked.

"Pardon?"

"Tic-Tac-Toe. It's great for passing the time. You are X, and I am O," Sarah said.

No matter how many times they played, Samuel always begged for another round.

When Sarah couldn't bear to play anymore, she sketched out a dirt hopscotch and numbered the squares.

When Samuel didn't recognize the shape, she knew she would have to teach him this game, too. Sarah picked up two pebbles and handed one to Samuel. She tossed her pebble into the first square and daintily hopped through the boxes on one foot, turned around and hopped back. She scooped up the pebble as she passed over square number one.

As Sarah tossed the pebble into the second square and hopped around, Samuel smiled. "It's your turn," she stepped back and grinned at Samuel.

Samuel threw the pebble into the first square.

"You can't step on the lines," she said as he took off on one foot. He jiggled, jumped, rested, jiggled, and wobbled around, with his arms flailing, as he made his way through the numbered squares.

"You're doing fine," she said, squelching her giggles.

Huffing and puffing, the stocky man bent over to pick up the pebble on one foot and rolled right over the last square, landing in a heap on the floor in front of Sarah. He gave out a loud belly laugh, and Sarah fell on the floor next to him, howling with laughter.

"That is quite enough exercise for me, Jeb." Panting, Samuel leaned his back against a stall board. "I've worked up an appetite. Might you like to join me, my friend?" Samuel yanked some bread and dried meat from his pocket and offered her some.

"Thank you, Samuel, but I have my own." She extracted a third of a biscuit and her half-eaten apple from her pocket. She started to take Miss Prickle out, but then remembered where she was. *I'm sorry Miss Prickle, you must stay put, for now*, she thought, as she gave the doll a gentle squeeze. Sarah and Samuel sat on the floor, munching and looking out at the rain. Sarah found herself thinking of Anna and how kind the young girl had been to her. She missed her constant chatter.

Culpepper slurped up the few crumbs they dropped, and Samuel fed him some meat.

"That is all for now, Culpepper." Samuel ran his hand across the pup's neck. "Well, it seems we shall be here for the evening, Jeb. You must prepare a bed for yourself in the hay."

"I'll take the horse stall. I guess that's what they mean when they say it's time to hit the hay." Sarah chuckled.

Samuel picked up Culpepper and climbed up into the hayloft. "See you on the morrow, my young friend."

"Goodnight, Samuel."

CHAPTER 13

Sarah dreamed that Jerome was tugging at her arm as she searched for her birthday present. When she awoke, Culpepper was tugging at her sleeve. Sarah rose, shooed the pup away, and dashed to the barn door.

"Samuel, come look! It's not raining!" Sarah cried as whitish-yellow sunbeams streamed in and danced through the barn. As she crossed the dirt floor, Culpepper ran to her and burrowed his snout into her jacket pocket. When he pulled his head out, he held Miss Prickle in his teeth. As Sarah tugged on the doll, Culpepper pulled on the doll the opposite way.

"Let go!" Sarah whispered. "Give it up!" She yanked at the doll. Rrrip! She cringed at the sound of cloth tearing apart before the dog released Miss Prickle.

"Gather your things and make haste, Jeb. We must set off." Samuel said, climbing down from the loft.

Sarah shoved Miss Prickle into her pocket. "Coming, Samuel." She scooped up her meager possessions and rushed out the door.

Sarah and Samuel inhaled the crisp morning air. They watched as mallard ducks dabbled in the pond under a bright blue, cloudless sky. As the sunshine warmed them, Sarah drew out a few large biscuit crumbs from her pocket and smooshed them together. She popped the blob into her mouth, as they walked over a rocky mound toward the road.

When Sarah reached into her pocket for Miss Prickle, her fingers landed on soft cotton stuffing. *Oh no! That pesky dog ripped Miss Prickle! He better stay away from me if he knows what's good for him!*

"Such a glorious morning, is it not?" Samuel said.

Sarah shrugged. "I guess."

"It is a blessing to escape from the horse sweat, don't you think?"

"Horse sweat's better than dog breath!"

Samuel shot a glance at Sarah. "Jeb, what's on your mind?"

Head down, eyes staring at the muddy road, Sarah kicked hard at a stone and sent it up the road. Samuel scurried ahead of her, found the stone, and gave it another boot. "Are you always this grumpy in the morning?" He panted.

When Sarah found the stone again in her path, she kicked it with all her might. "Only when nosey little dogs don't mind their own business."

Samuel went racing by her to retrieve the stone. He found it and kicked it back into her path. "Did Culpepper get into something he should not have?"

Sarah came to a halt and faced Samuel. "Yeah, you could say that." Sarah could feel the anger rising in her throat. Her lower lip quivered as she fought back the tears. She balled her hands into fists and squeezed them hard to control herself. Yanking on the brim of her hat to cover her eyes, she lowered her head and kept walking. She found the same rock and gave it one final swift kick propelling it far from the path. Sarah stared at Samuel, daring him to go after it.

The man ignored it and just kept walking. After a long pause, he spoke. "Lad, I have a way with words. I can make them jump off the pages, and I can anger crowds to take action. Some call me *The Great Agitator*." Samuel chuckled. "Do you know what an agitator is, Jeb?" Sarah shook her head and thrust out her lower lip. "It's someone who stirs up others. I had no idea that Culpepper was following in my footsteps," he said, smiling. "However, the one ability that I do not possess is to mindread, and you've noticed Culpepper cannot speak, so please tell me what he did."

Sarah looked into Samuel's laughing eyes, reached into her pocket and drew out Miss Prickle.

Samuel's eyes moved to the doll. "A poppet, is it?"

"Yeah, uh...my sister, Sarah, put it in my pocket before I left. She thought it would bring me good luck." Sarah looked down and moved some mud with her shoe. "Culpepper tore it. What will I tell her when I return?"

"Let me have her, Jeb. I will mend her." Samuel sat on a nearby rock, opened the leather pouch fastened to his waist and drew out a large needle and a thin piece of twine. Pushing the stuffing back into the doll's stomach, Samuel closed the doll's wound with five tiny stitches. He held Miss Prickle up. "There she is. Good as new." He handed the doll to Sarah.

"My sister won't even notice," Sarah grinned, as she smoothed out Miss Prickle's dress and shoved her back into her pocket.

"Culpepper, stay away from things that do not belong to you," Samuel said, wagging his stubby finger at the dog.

"Yes, Culpepper. That goes for me, too. You little agitator."

The dog wagged his tail and came bounding into its owner's lap.

Sarah laughed.

The threesome traveled onward. Sarah's stomach ached from hunger, and her throat was parched.

A mile up the path, Samuel said, "My friend's farmhouse is nearby. It is in our best interest to impose upon Stephen for a good breakfast." Sarah grinned and speeded up.

"How much further?" she asked, as a fluffy-tailed gray squirrel ran across her path.

"Oh, just a hop, skip and a jump down the road," he said, hopping, skipping and then jumping as Sarah laughed and mimicked him.

Before long, a small, red farmhouse came into view. A thin swirl of smoke rose from its chimney.

"If I know Stephen, he is just sitting down to breakfast. If we are lucky, it is one that we will share."

What would my mother say about showing up uninvited and begging for food? Sarah thought. "Is this a good idea, Samuel? He's not expecting us."

"Why, it's a brilliant idea! My stomach thinks so, too." He patted his midsection.

Sarah grinned and threw out her little belly. "So does mine!" she chirped, patting her stomach.

Samuel winked at her and with Culpepper at his heels, boldly stepped up onto his friend's wide, welcoming front porch and knocked on the door of the simple, brown farmhouse.

A gray and white striped cat, busy sunning itself, darted for cover under a nearby rhododendron bush. The door opened, and there stood a tall, barrel-chested man with a long horsey face. He had dark, wavy hair and a smattering of freckles across the bridge of his wide nose. Upon glimpsing Samuel, his face broke into a giant-sized grin. Two long arms embraced Samuel and lifted him off the ground in a rib-compressing bear hug. Both men emitted loud whoops and kicked their feet around in joy. When Stephen finally released Samuel, he gave him a hearty slap across the back.

"And who might this be?" Stephen said, noticing wide-eyed Sarah drinking in the enthusiastic greeting.

"Forgive me, Stephen. This is my traveling companion, Jebediah Horatio Atkins. Jeb, may I present to you my friend, Mr. Stephen Atherton."

Stephen bowed with a flourish and extended his hand to Sarah. "I am most honored to make your acquaintance, sir. You must be quite a noble young man for Mr. Samuel Adams to choose you as his traveling companion."

Sarah gawked at Samuel as she felt her body electrify. *Samuel Adams! The Samuel Adams? The leader of the Sons of Liberty?* She thought. She could barely contain herself. *Now it all makes sense. Of course, he's on his way to the meeting. He's probably running the meeting!* Sarah stood speechless.

Stephen turned to Samuel again. "'Tis a blessing to have you here. Your timing is splendid. I was just sitting down to morning meal, so my friends, you shall join me and bring me abreast of the goings on in the taverns of Boston."

"If you have ample to share, Jeb and I could be persuaded." Samuel winked at Sarah and removed his hat. "Jeb, shall we take Stephen up on his generous offer?"

Sarah blinked. "What?" she was still dumbfounded that she was traveling with the great Samuel Adams.

"Shall we stay for a meal?"

"Um ... yes ... whatever you say." Sarah's stomach had done such a flip-flop in the past few moments that she didn't know if she could eat one bite, but she knew that Samuel was hungry.

"Then it is settled," Stephen said. "Pull that bench over, Jebediah." Stephen laid out two more trenchers and placed a large skillet with thick, crisp slices of sizzling bacon in front of them. He retrieved a large piece for each of his guests and served both of them a buttery, warm biscuit to go with it.

"Jeb, are you forgetting your manners?" Samuel stared at Sarah's hat.

Sarah's eyes met her friend's. She then looked over at Stephen who was waiting for her to take her cap off. Sarah's hands went up to her hat. She touched the soft felt wondering what the men would do when they found out she was a girl.

"I'm still cold. Do you know that eighty percent of your body heat escapes through your head? A hat prevents that," Sarah said. Ignoring the puzzled looks on the men's faces, she shoved a big piece of bacon into her mouth. The men glared at her as she chomped her food.

Without a word, Stephen reached for the kettle that was warming on the fireplace and poured a sweet-smelling brown liquid into his tin cup. Samuel took a long swallow, wiped the lip of the cup with his shirtsleeve and passed it to Sarah. She sniffed it and then took a small sip. *Apple cider, just like on Halloween!* Sarah thought. She took a couple more sips, wiped the edge of the cup, and passed it back to their host. It was Stephen who finally broke the silence.

"Tell me, Samuel, what is the scuttlebutt from the taverns of Massachusetts?"

Sarah kept her eyes on her plate.

"No doubt you have been informed of the dreadful Stamp Tax."

"Surely, I have, as have all the colonists in Connecticut. The economy is not bad enough without England sticking her hand out, once again. First, it is The Sugar Act; now it is The Stamp Act. If we continue to give in, their demands will be endless."

"The King has commissioned Jared Ingersoll, a New Haven magistrate, as a collection agent for these taxes. A scoundrel, he is!" Stephen said, pounding the table with his fist.

Culpepper began to bark. "And our spineless Governor Fitch is allowing it!" Stephan's face flushed as Samuel nodded. "Not one stamp will *this* man purchase." He thrummed his chest. "England has gotten enough gifts from her American colonists!"

"My friend, you speak like an orator. Come with us to the meeting in New Haven and share your energy."

"Ah, the planting season is so short, that I am afraid I cannot. But my prayers will follow you and Jeb," Stephen said.

After all the bacon had been eaten, Stephen drained the fat from the skillet and fried the eggs. Despite eating with her hands, Sarah had never tasted breakfast as scrumptious as that morning she shared bacon and eggs with Samuel Adams and his friend, Stephen.

"If Jeb and I are to reach New Haven by nightfall, we must make haste," Samuel said as he rose and motioned to Sarah. When Culpepper appeared at Samuel's side, Stephan tossed the dog a biscuit.

"We are grateful for breakfast, and it was nice to meet you, Mr. Atherton," Sarah said, extending her hand.

"Perhaps next time, you will not feel so cold, my friend," Stephen said, winking at Sarah. When he tugged on the brim of her cap, Sarah grabbed both sides, shoved the cap down over her ears and looked down.

"Stop by on your journey back, my friends." Stephen waved as Sarah, Samuel, and Culpepper disappeared down the road.

CHAPTER 14

None of the kids at school will believe this. I played Tic-Tac-Toe and Hopscotch with Samuel Adams! Sarah thought as she walked down the dirt road with the sun warming her back.

"Jeb, you are getting thoughtful on me again," Samuel said.

"I guess I just ran out of things to say."

"I see. But if you are troubled by something, you will tell me, won't you?"

"Sure, Samuel."

Samuel started to whistle, and before long Sarah joined him. They sauntered down a winding dirt road under a canopy of shade trees.

"Where did you learn to whistle?" Samuel asked.

"My father."

"Tell me about your father, Jeb. Is he a blacksmith?"

"No. My father...uh ... he's at home right now."

"Ah, he works the land," Samuel smiled.

Sarah gave a half smile in return. "Samuel, why didn't you tell me your last name when we first met?"

Samuel's eyebrows shot up. "Why that is truly an odd question, my friend." He shrugged his shoulders. "It's not important. I am merely Samuel to my friends."

"Of course, it's important! *You* are very important and I might have... Well, maybe I would have acted differently if I knew you were Samuel Adams."

"I am just an ordinary man who enjoys creating a little controversy. It entertains me to make people think. If you *did* know my last name, how would you have treated me? Would you have forced me out of the barn back into the rain?"

"Oh, no!" Sarah said.

"Would you have refused to share your biscuit with Culpepper?"

"Of course not!"

"Oh, I know. You wouldn't have taught me Tic-Tac-Toe or Hop the Scotch! That is it!"

Sarah giggled.

"Jeb, what have I done to make you so ill at ease?"

Sarah faced her friend and drew in a deep breath. "If I knew you were Samuel Adams from Boston, great writer, leader of The Sons of Liberty movement, second cousin of John Adams, one of our Pres— Oh no!" Sarah slapped her hand across her mouth and stared at the perplexed look on Samuel's face. Samuel narrowed his eyes at Sarah and shook his head in disbelief.

"Where did you learn of this? I haven't relayed this to you."

"I…I have heard others talk about you. And I have a good memory."

"I see."

"I'm just saying that if I knew who you were, I would have been more respectful."

"Jeb, you have been very respectful. I do not know how you know so much about me, but you give me too much credit. There are those who admire me and those loyal to the King who do not. You see, I do enjoy humor at King George's expense, besides not agreeing with him on some policies. And when tempers flare up over my political antics, I hide out for a time until the unrest settles. If it were not for men like Stephen Atherton who take me in, I would be sitting in the lockup on Boston Common."

"But what you write about makes such perfect sense, Samuel. Your friend, Mr. Atherton has the right idea. If you..." Sarah stopped herself. "I mean... if *we* stand by and let England tax us, we will lose everything everyone has worked so hard for."

"You are correct, Jeb."

"Whoa, what have we here?" Samuel stopped short. A knee-high mass of intertwined, heavy tree limbs, rotted logs, and bramble bushes blocked their way.

"Will we be able to get around it?"

"Watch where I step and follow me," Samuel said. Slowly and surely, they worked their way through Mother Nature's clutter.

"Samuel, getting back to what I was saying, why don't colonists stand up for what they think is right? What are they afraid of?"

"People are afraid if they speak out, Parliament will take away our charter. What many colonists do not understand is that England has already broken the agreement with us by taxing us. The charter reads that we have 'an exclusive right to make laws for our own internal government and taxation.'"

"And what does that mean, Samuel?"

"It means that the colonies are allowed to set up their own rules of government and their own taxation system without interference from England. England broke the rules by taxing us, so she forfeits her rights."

"What were her rights?" Sarah asked.

"To treat us as loyal subjects of the King and to profit from our prosperity," Samuel said.

"So, what happens now?"

"Another good question, my friend. Up until now, we have had our governors composing letters to Parliament to state our reasons for disagreeing with the policy. I'm afraid now; sterner measures are in order. That is why we must meet in New Haven." Samuel stopped and pointed to the ground. "Hmm, it looks like a bear track."

"W-W-What? Did you say a bear track?"

"Yes, a fresh one, too. We are getting close to the river. He's probably planning on doing some fishing. We shall keep an eye open for him."

Sarah moved closer to Samuel, shooting intermittent glances over her shoulders.

As the road narrowed and rose to an incline, Samuel's breath rattled in his throat. Beads of sweat formed on his top lip and forehead. He wiped his brow on his sleeve. "Enough of this talk. I must rest my weary bones. There is a bend in the river that passes not far from here. I think it is time I rest and freshen my face." He rubbed his hand across his whiskers.

"Uh, me too." Sarah stroked her chin.

Samuel's eyes twinkled, and he broke into a grin." Follow me."

Samuel and Sarah left the road. As they weaved through a cluster of pine trees, they heard the roar of water rushing over rocks. "The river has risen considerably. We must find a more placid area," Samuel said as he looked around. "That way." He pointed north.

They came upon a fallen tree. As its roots still clung to the shore, its wide trunk and branches blocked the flow of the river and created a tranquil, little pool. Samuel removed his hat, kneeled down and splashed the cool water across his face and over his head.

"Brr! Refreshing for the soul!" He cupped his hands, scooped up some water and gulped it down. He then swished the water across his teeth, threw his head back and gargled. Opening his leather pouch, he pulled out a long, straight-edged razor. As Culpepper frolicked and Sarah looked on, Samuel scraped the protruding hairs from his chin and upper lip. "Will you not be refreshing yourself, Jeb? Cleanliness is next to Godliness, I daresay."

Sarah walked a ways downstream, pushed back the brim of her hat, washed her face and drank her fill. She swished some water around her mouth and let out a noisy gurgle to alert Samuel that she was freshening up.

When Sarah finished washing, she headed back and found Samuel sprawled out against a tree stump, the brim of his hat pulled down across his eyes. Culpepper had curled up beside him. Sarah walked over to them, took off her jacket, and stretched out. The sun felt good on her face as she stared up into the spring sky. Light, fluffy clouds floated overhead as a gentle breeze pushed them along. It was good to stretch out and relax after all the walking she had done, but Sarah wasn't sleepy.

Yesterday, I was a runaway with no particular destination. Today I'm Samuel Adams' traveling companion on my way to a Sons of Liberty meeting in New Haven! What a difference a day makes, she thought.

But still, she worried about would happen when they got to New Haven. Sarah wished she had a good friend to talk to. She felt inside her pocket and gave Miss Prickle a gentle squeeze. "Don't lose hope," she whispered to the doll.

Suddenly, she heard a low snort. Samuel was snoring. Culpepper woke up and bounded over. He jumped up on her chest and started licking her face. "Yuk! Dog germs!" Sarah laughed. She reached for a small stick and pitched it. "Fetch, doggie, fetch," she said as she threw the stick.

The dog just sat.

She retrieved the stick and let Culpepper smell it. She placed the stick in front of Culpepper's nose, letting him get a good sniff and then pitched it. "Go get it, boy."

The dog looked at her but didn't move. He wagged his tail; a dripping pink tongue hung out over his teeth.

"Go get it."

The dog still didn't budge.

Sarah picked up the stick and stuck it near Culpepper's mouth and watched as he licked it.

When she flung it again, Culpepper sailed over to the stick, picked it up in his teeth, and returned it to Sarah.

"Good doggie! Good doggie!" She grabbed the neck of the dog and gave him a hard squeeze.

Culpepper licked her face, barked, and wagged his tail.

"What in tarnation is going on?" asked Samuel. "Cannot a man enjoy a short rest?"

"Watch, Samuel. I taught Culpepper how to fetch." Sarah held the stick to the dog's nose and yelled "Fetch!" just before she released it into the air. The pup bounded after it and returned it to Sarah.

"Well, I'll be! I thought the only trick that scamp knew was how to beg food." Sarah handed the stick to Samuel.

"You do it. Let him smell it."

The man let the dog sniff the stick, and then tossed it high into the air. While it was still airborne, Culpepper leaped and caught it in his teeth. Samuel watched with wide eyes, then clapped and hooted when the dog returned the stick to him. Samuel picked up the stick once again and tossed it high into the air. The dog caught it mid-flight but skidded off the bank and slid into the river with the stick still in his teeth. Before Samuel and Sarah realized what had happened, Culpepper was being carried downriver in the quick current.

"Culpepper! Culpepper!" Samuel shouted. But it was too late. The dog was no match for the force of the water.

Both Samuel and Sarah were off in a flash, racing to keep the dog in sight. The river wound around and started to slow. Now downriver, they spotted the dog coming towards them, heading toward a cluster of rocks.

"Samuel, he's coming this way. Swim out and get him before he gets smashed in the rocks!" Sarah yelled.

Huffing and puffing, Samuel stopped short. "It would not be wise to challenge the river, Jeb. The current is too powerful, and I do not swim. I am afraid Culpepper is on his own."

Sarah looked at Samuel's anguished face. She turned back to the yelping pup heading for the rocks.

She kicked off her shoes and ripped off her jacket. *Excess clothing becomes heavy when wet;* she remembered Coach Farrell's words.

"Oh, no! Jeb, w-w-what are you doing? Stop this...you are *not* going after him!" Samuel moved towards Sarah and grabbed her arm.

"Don't worry. I'm a trained swimmer. I won't do anything foolish." Sarah broke free and ran towards the water. She jumped into the frigid, waist-high water with a splash. Her whole body trembled as Samuel stared at her. "Take off your jacket, Samuel!" She shouted.

Samuel did as he was told.

"Now tie one of the sleeves to one of my jacket sleeves."

He tied the sleeves together.

Sarah looked back into the water and Culpepper had hit the clump of rocks just where she thought he would. The dog was frightened, and his drenched body was being tossed and thrown against the rocks. *If he could just push away from those rocks and float into the deeper water, I could reach him,* she thought.

Sarah turned back to Samuel. His wide face was somber as he watched his pet battered by the churning water. "Take your shoes off and follow me, Samuel. Bring the jackets and walk into the water as far as you can without losing your footing."

Samuel followed Sarah's instructions.

Sarah knew she could not afford to stay in the cold water for too long. By the time Samuel walked in as far as he dared, Sarah had already started to tread water. "I'm going to take one end of the jacket, and you hold the other. Whatever you do, don't let go!"

Samuel nodded and watched as Sarah swam out as far as the jackets would stretch. The dog thrashed back and forth in the rocks.

As the current pushed against her, she yelled, "Culpepper! Culpepper! Come here, boy!"

The dog yelped but refused to leave the security of the rocks.

If Sarah could only convince the dog to fetch, she might be able to get him away from the rocks. She looked around for something floating by that would have enough weight to throw. She couldn't reach anything. Then she remembered Miss Prickle. She reached her arm into the pocket of her jacket and grabbed Miss Prickle's wooden head. She grasped the wet doll in her hands. *Should I take the chance? What if Culpepper won't fetch? What if I lose her forever?*

Culpepper's desperate bark confirmed the correct decision.

Sarah held the doll high above her head. "Culpepper! Culpepper! Fetch, boy! Fetch!" She flung the doll upstream just in front of the rocks. "Fetch!" Sarah pointed to the doll. Sarah waited and watched as the wooden doll head bobbed downstream just beyond her reach. "Nooo, Miss Prickle," whispered Sarah, shaking her head as she helplessly watched the doll float away. Sarah glared at the dog. "Culpepper, you fetch that doll now!"

"Jeb, come back. You have done your best." Samuel called.

Sarah turned towards Samuel's sad face. They were both losing their most prized possessions, he his dog, and she her doll. Sarah started to cry just as she heard a bark. Through a blur of tears, she saw the pup come from around the rocks and paddle after her doll. Sarah got back into position. She watched as the dog swam toward her with Miss Prickle in his teeth.

"Yes! Good doggie, good boy, Culpepper," she coaxed. When he got close, she reached out and scooped him up in her arms.

In his eagerness, Culpepper jumped on Sarah's shoulders and forced her head under water. Sarah emerged coughing and sputtering and watched as the current pushed her hat down the river.

Samuel gaped at Sarah's face and wet braids. His jaw dropped, and for an instant, man and girl stared into each other's eyes.

"Pull, Samuel. Pull us in." Samuel tugged with both hands and the shivering, sopping duo crawled onto the river bank and collapsed. Sarah thought about fleeing, but she couldn't move.

Samuel stared at Sarah, a look of amazement on his face. Water dripped from her long, brown braids.

For a long time, there was no sound except for the rustling of leaves. Then, Samuel spoke. "You certainly are full of surprises, Jeb, or whatever your name might be. We had best be on our way if we are to dry out before we reach New Haven." Samuel walked back to the spot where he had left his leather bag.

Teeth chattering, Sarah squeezed out the excess water from Miss Prickle and then squeezed the water out of her own hair. She caught up to Samuel. "Samuel, I'm sorry. I should have told you. I just don't know who to trust anymore."

"It appears you have no choice now, but to trust me." He yanked on his boots. Sarah quickly laced up her shoes. "I ought to have been suspicious from the beginning, a Negro *alone* on an errand. And you, so attached to that hat of yours. Come along. We are going to New Haven." He glared at her bare head. "And by the looks of it, you are in need of this." He placed his hat on her head. The large-brimmed hat fell over her ears. She swooped up her braids and tucked them inside.

"Thanks." Sarah gave an awkward grin.

"Well, one good turn deserves another, I suppose. Thank you for saving Culpepper, Jeb. I mean...Sarah. That is your name is it not? The name on the poppet?"

"Yes, that really *is* my name. And I am *not* a runaway slave. I'm just a normal girl with an unbelievable story."

"Well, I daresay you are not a *normal* girl, but I think we have time for one more unbelievable story before we reach New Haven." Samuel gathered up the rest of his things, motioned to Culpepper, and the three set off for the last leg of their journey.

CHAPTER 15

The trio was only a short distance from New Haven, and Sarah's story had been told. Samuel remained particularly quiet throughout the telling. "So, Samuel, you have to believe me. And don't send me back to the Ruggles. Please?"

Samuel gave a long sigh. "Sarah, I do not doubt that you honestly believe what you have just told me, yet sometimes the mind plays tricks on us. I can see you have quite an imagination. Perhaps you will learn to write stories as well as you read and swim."

"Samuel, I know that I can't figure out how I got here, but I know I don't belong here. I truly *am* from another time, the twenty-first century, and I don't belong in the 1700s."

Samuel furrowed his brow. "What you are telling me is preposterous."

"You are going to New Haven to convince people that it's wrong for England to place taxes on the colonies with no representation in Parliament. Will Paul Revere and John Hancock be at your meeting?"

"How do you know those names?"

"I told you, I've read about them. Paul is a silversmith from Boston. He's a great patriot who will ride his horse to warn the colonial militia that the British are coming before the first war shots ring out in Lexington and Concord. John Hancock, a great statesman, will be the first man to sign the Declaration of Independence when you break away from England. He's a showoff and will make his signature very large so the King won't miss it. There will be a tremendous revolution in the colonies, but the good news is that thirteen colonies will band together to establish what will one day be the United States of America!"

Samuel said nothing.

"So, who do you think will be there?"

"I...uh...don't quite know whom to expect, possibly Oliver Wolcott from Litchfield."

"Hmm. I don't know that name."

"And Mr. Arnold. He lives in New Haven." Samuel said.

"Arnold? You mean Benedict Arnold?"

"Why, yes."

"Watch out for him. He's a traitor!"

"Sarah, stop! Mr. Arnold is a respected pharmacist and bookseller. I'll not have you speaking ill of him."

Sarah turned away.

"Very well then, I believe I have heard enough. Under the circumstances, perhaps you and your imagination should return to Boston with me after this meeting, and I will see to it that you are quartered with a caring family. My dear Elizabeth and I cannot afford to feed another mouth," Samuel said.

As Sarah hung her head and considered that she would soon leave Connecticut behind to grow up in Boston, Culpepper started to yap. A village green, littered with geese, pigs and sheep came into view. There were two brick buildings. The large one had a tower on it, and the smaller was surrounded by a crowd of people.

As they got closer, Sarah spotted a wooden wagon being dragged by a team of oxen across a crisscrossed dirt path. Carts filled with fish, tools and leather goods were set up on the southernmost end of the green, and townsfolk bustled about buying, trading, and haggling. The elm trees and homes that lined the common were much larger than those in Guilford, and Sarah was struck by the fact that almost all the houses were a light blue in color. Tucked behind the building where the crowd had assembled was an overcrowded, neglected cemetery enclosed by a broad, bright, red fence.

"Go back where you came from, Mr. Ingersoll! We'll not listen to you or your directives!" A tall red-headed man screamed and stormed out from the middle of a crowd of townspeople. Chattering erupted from the people around him.

"Stay here, Sarah," Samuel ordered. He and Culpepper charged into the fray.

Too curious to stay behind, Sarah moved toward the disturbance and threaded her way through the throng. She stood on tiptoes and craned her neck to catch a glimpse of the action and followed Culpepper's high-pitched bark as it rang out above the shouts.

Amidst the crowd, Sarah spied a man perched atop a skittish brown steed. He wore a dark blue, double-breasted uniform, with glistening brass buttons and highly polished black boots. "I understand how angered you must be, my friends; however, the King has entrusted me as the agent for the stamps," he said. "I am obligated to perform my duties."

The crowd jeered.

"Go away, or we'll send you away tarred and feathered!" A portly man called out.

"Gentlemen, ladies, calm yourselves," Samuel said. "Good fellow, we mean you no harm, but Britain granted us a charter which provided that we, the colonists, make our own laws and levy our own taxes. Not only is the Crown denying us our charter, but we are being deprived of representation in Parliament! Shall we have no say in how we are governed?"

"No taxation without representation!" the crowd chanted.

I can't believe I'm here! This isn't some class play! I'm actually part of the challenge to King George! Sarah thought as she was jostled by the heated crowd.

"Does England pay the colonies a fee when we send our quilts, shoes, and ironworks to Dover?" Samuel asked.

"No!" The crowd shouted.

"Sir, advise the King that we shall not accept his stamps. The time has come to say no taxation without representation!" Samuel shouted, as the crowd, including Sarah, clapped and cheered.

"And who might I name as the bold man who sent me back to the King with this information, sir?"

"My name is Samuel Adams of Boston, and these good people are the proud colonists of Connecticut!" Samuel fanned his hands across the crowd.

Whistles and shouts rang out.

"Take our message to the King!" a wiry man with a weathered face screamed.

"Take our message to the King!" a plump woman with a child on her hip shouted.

As Sarah grinned at the woman's boldness, everyone cheered and clapped harder than ever. Culpepper, who had sniffed out Sarah, barked and wagged his tail. Sarah beamed at Samuel and then turned to the jubilant faces of the townspeople.

A lone male voice rose from the crowd. "Take our message to the King! Take our message to the King!"

Several more voices chimed in. "Take our message to the King!" The voices grew stronger. Before long the entire group was chanting. "Take our message to the King! Take our message to the King!"

As the color drained from the face of the King's tax collector, his horse reared up. It galloped off through the jeering mob, while people quickly dove to the left and right to clear the way. Gleeful men clustered around Samuel, laughing, smiling, and slapping him on the back.

"Let that loyalist go back to England!" one of the men scoffed.

It struck Sarah as funny, and she started to giggle. She bent over to pick up Culpepper, and he wagged his tail and licked her face.

"It would be my pleasure to buy you a cup of ale, Mr. Adams. I believe the tavern is open for business," a stranger said.

Samuel grinned at the invitation. He looked around and spotted Sarah with Culpepper. "I thought I told you to stay put," he growled.

Sarah's eyes searched the ground.

Samuel sighed and shook his head. "Well, what do you say we go over to the tavern?"

"Sure," said Sarah who had never been inside a bar before and had often wondered what one looked like.

Samuel, Sarah, Culpepper, and the admiring stranger strode toward a large stone house with a wrap-around porch and four massive chimneys. A sign hung above the wide front door. It read *Beers Inn and Tavern.*

When they arrived at the front door, Samuel turned to Sarah and pointed to a wooden stool on the front porch. "You and Culpepper are to stay here. I will not be long."

Sarah gave him a long look as he disappeared through the doors with his new friends at his side. A few minutes later he came back out and placed a mug in Sarah's hands. "Sarsaparilla for my young friend."

Sarah smiled in appreciation and sipped the refreshing drink. Samuel disappeared once again through the tavern doors. Sarah removed her jacket, spread it out on the bench and propped up Miss Prickle next to her. She stretched her legs out and leaned back on the bench watching the townsfolk.

Culpepper found a small puddle and was busy draining it dry. A small, red, horse-drawn coach pulled up in front of the tavern. Its doors were white and trimmed with shiny brass. There were two large wagon wheels in the back and two smaller ones in the front. The horses were blinkered, and a large trunk and small box were attached to the back of the coach with three wide leather straps.

As a well-dressed couple emerged, Sarah strained to see inside the vehicle and spotted two brown leather seats, facing each other, and highly polished wooden floorboards.

"Hello," Sarah said as the couple rushed by her and headed for the tavern. Sarah sat on the front porch day-dreaming about how her life had changed in the past few days and how it would change even more when Samuel's meeting was over. She had decided she would take his offer to return to Boston with him. She didn't want to leave Connecticut, but she didn't have a choice. She knew she couldn't continue alone. *Besides, I can be useful to him. I know how history plays out for the colonists. I could be his trusted adviser if I could just get him to believe what I tell him,* she thought.

As Sarah sat on the front porch of the tavern staring out across the green, considering her future, two boys scampered by playing hit the hoop. She thought back to the other day and remembered how embarrassed she was when Mrs. Ruggles had scolded her in front of all the other kids. Now, a young blond boy was so intent on keeping the hoop rolling that he charged into an unsuspecting villager, knocking his hat off.

"You don't belong here menacing the patrons of this tavern," the man shook a stern finger.

Sarah squinted to get a better look at him. There was something vaguely familiar about him. As he bent over to pick up his hat, Sarah realized she was staring at none other than Mr. Nathaniel Hill!

Uh, oh! I've got to get out of here! she thought. She threw on her jacket, stuffed Miss Prickle into her pocket and yanked Samuel's cap down over her ears. As she turned around, pretending to look through the tavern window, Mr. Hill passed to her left and opened the front door. Sarah smelled the stench of stale beer and heard the raucous laughter of the men at the bar.

She peered through the window to try to spot Samuel. Knowing that Hill was in the tavern, Sarah started to pace back and forth on the front porch. *Come on, Samuel, hurry up*, she thought.

Every time the door opened, Sarah turned her back so that no one coming or going could see her face. Finally, Samuel stepped out of the tavern. As soon as Sarah realized it was he, she jumped to his side.

"You seem a bit skittish," he said.

"That dreadful Mr. Hill who beat me and locked me up is inside. Let's get out of here."

"He must have come into town for the meeting tomorrow," Samuel said as Culpepper scampered up to them, happy to see his master once again. He tossed the dog a large soup bone.

The door to the tavern swung open once again and out stepped the man who had offered Samuel the drink.

"Thank you again, Simon, for the refreshment."

"It was my pleasure, good sir. Where are you off to now?"

"My companion and I will be looking for lodging for this evening. Do you know of anyone who might need some boarders?"

Simon looked at Sarah. "Is the boy honest?"

"Naturally. I would have it no other way."

Simon smiled. "Then I would be honored if you and your friend would stay with Mistress Tuttle and me. By the looks of it, you two could use a good meal."

Samuel and Sarah exchanged looks of relief. They followed as Simon led the way to his house.

CHAPTER 16

Simon Tuttle was true to his word. He led Samuel to his chamber and offered Sarah a comfortable attic room with a jack bed covered with a goose down comforter. They both slept well and woke refreshed.

When she dressed for breakfast, Sarah was happy to see that her clothes were almost completely dry. She kept Samuel's hat on except when she slept, and thus had to endure disapproving looks from her hosts.

The brick courthouse that had been the site of yesterday's disturbance was where the meeting was scheduled. Simon, Samuel, and Sarah set off after breakfast, Culpepper at their heels. As they approached the courthouse, Sarah noticed an ugly old whipping post and hurried past it.

People were already starting to arrive, most of them men. Some pulled up in carriages, some on horseback, but most arrived on foot. The bells from the courthouse sounded as more and more people arrived.

As the threesome walked through the heavy wooden door, Samuel whispered to Sarah, "Sit in the back, close to the door, and keep a watchful eye on Culpepper."

Sarah was thrilled to be able to witness the action. She set Culpepper in her lap and anxiously awaited the beginning of the meeting. The courthouse bells finally stopped pealing, and a man who was seated near her got up and closed the large door.

I can't believe I'm really here at a meeting of the Sons of Liberty! she thought. Sarah beamed as her friend, Samuel, walked confidently up to a raised platform and addressed the assembly.

"My fellow Sons and Daughters of Liberty, thank you for joining together this day to discuss the impending Stamp Tax on the colonies. Most of you are aware, I am sure, that our governors have been corresponding with England for months. There is no indication that England will give us representation in Parliament if we give in to this Stamp Tax. It is inevitable it will be levied on us in the very near future."

The crowd murmured.

"Mr. Jared Ingersoll, with whom I had a confrontation yesterday, has informed us that he has been commissioned to collect the tax from this colony. There will be other agents sent by the King to do the same in other colonies. Of this, I am completely certain."

More grumblings from the crowd. Then there came a pounding on the courthouse door. A man rushed to open it, and in shuffled a red-faced Mr. Hill.

Oh no, it's him! Sarah panicked and slid down in her chair. She eyed Hill from under the brim of the hat.

Unable to find a seat, Hill stood off to the side. Sarah strained to concentrate on the speech, but she started to tremble, her legs jumped with nerves, and she felt nauseous.

I gotta get outta here! she thought, biting her lip.

"Your good Governor Fitch," came Samuel's voice once again, "has tried to persuade the King not to levy this tax. However, like Ingersoll, he would rather go along with it than to take a firm stand. That is what we are here for this day, my good people of Connecticut. We must decide what stand we will take against this tyranny."

"No stamps for Connecticut! Ingersoll be hanged!" came a voice from the middle of the room.

The crowd broke out once again in a thunderous chant, "No stamps for Connecticut! No stamps for Connecticut!"

Culpepper started to bark at all the excitement. He jumped off of Sarah's lap and went yelping down the aisle to where Samuel was.

Samuel raised his hand "Simmer down, my good people!" When order was restored, he searched for Sarah. "Jeb, come get Culpepper."

Sarah felt all eyes on her as she came up to the front and grabbed the pup. She lifted him into her arms and proceeded back to her seat. By the time Sarah had weaved her way back to her seat, it was already occupied by none other than Mr. Hill, who acknowledged her return with a smug smile. Their eyes met for a brief moment. Hill's cold steel eyes tore into Sarah's. Sarah immediately searched for the door. She ran up to it, Culpepper still in her arms, and pushed the heavy door open with the right side of her body.

She raced down the courthouse steps, past the whipping post, and went charging toward the marketplace searching for a secure hiding place. It didn't take long for Hill to remember the owner of those wide brown eyes that stared back at him. He raced out of the courthouse after her.

"Stop! Stop that Negro!" he shouted as he went barreling after her. "Stop that runaway!"

Sarah flew into a group of people milling around in the marketplace. When they heard Hill's shouts and saw him in hot pursuit, they joined the chase. More shouts followed, and Hill's posse grew. Before Sarah knew what had happened, she was cornered, and once again face-to-face with the hate-filled Nathaniel Hill.

As Hill advanced on Sarah, Culpepper growled and bared his teeth. Mr. Hill reached into his pocket and pulled out his club. He took a hard swipe at the pup and sent him flying.

"Leave him alone, you lousy creep!" Sarah screamed as she charged into Hill.

As soon as she did, she knew it was a mistake. She was trapped in his grip, kicking and screaming to escape. With all the pulling and tugging, Miss Prickle fell out of Sarah's pocket. She quickly swooped her up and stuffed her back in. Hill grabbed her and pulled off her hat, releasing the long brown braids for all to see.

The group of onlookers gasped. "Oh, it's a Negress!"

"Your pretentions are finished, missy," growled Hill. "And your punishment shall be swift and severe." He dragged Sarah back in the direction of the whipping post.

"Leave me alone, you miserable man!" Sarah stomped on his foot.

"You, young man," he pointed to a boy, watching with wide eyes. "Go fetch the town watchman and tell him to bring a strong whip."

"Yes, sir." The boy ran off.

"What is her crime?" a curious spectator asked.

"She is a runaway and a thief," Hill replied.

"You're lying. I didn't steal anything!"

"Very well then, check her pocket." Hill pointed to her pocket. I believe you will find a stolen poppet."

A red-haired woman reached inside Sarah's pocket and drew out Miss Prickle for all to see. "Gracious! The Negress *is* a thief! She deserves a good thrashing indeed."

"That's my doll! My father gave her to me. Give her back," Sarah lunged for the doll.

Mr. Hill grabbed Sarah and got her into a headlock.

"I daresay a servant would not possess such a lovely poppet. The girl is a thief!" the woman cried, as she helped Hill drag Sarah toward the whipping post.

Sarah struggled even harder, but it was impossible for her to break loose. "Samuel! Help me, Samuel!"

"No one will hear you, and no one will dare to interfere with your punishment," Hill grunted.

Sarah began to cry as the boy returned with a whip.

"The town watchman is in the meeting and does not wish to be disturbed, sir."

"Then I will need to administer her flogging myself." He threw her against the post, drew up both her arms above her head, and fastened the leather straps around her wrists.

Defeated and embarrassed by all the eyes on her, Sarah started to cry. *I can't believe this is happening!* She thought. *Where is Samuel?* Her frightened brown eyes pleaded for the courthouse doors to open. She searched the crowd for a sympathetic face. Through her tears, she caught sight of Miss Prickle, still in the woman's hands.

Hill made a couple of showy strikes in the air with the whip.

"Give me my doll! I want my doll!" She screamed through her tears.

"The poppet will be returned to its proper owner, child." The woman folded Miss Prickle into her cloak.

Sarah sobbed in complete frustration and braced herself for the whip.

"My dear woman, kindly give me the poppet." Hill reached out his hand.

As the woman handed over the poppet to him, the doors to the courthouse opened wide. Sarah screamed. "Samuel! Help me!"

Hill knew he had little time to spare when he saw the townspeople drift out of the courthouse. A monstrous sneer crossed his face.

Sarah closed her eyes tightly and braced herself for Hill's first strike.

"You want the doll? Take her!" With the full force of his right hand, Hill hurled the doll at Sarah and raised his whip.

As the doll crashed against the wooden whipping post, the sky darkened. A tremendous gust of wind whipped up. Hill's hat flew off and the bystanders scattered. Debris flew all around, and Miss Prickle crashed at the base of the post. The straps that held Sarah's hands in place tore and fell away. Sarah reached for her doll and then collapsed at the base of the post. A flash of light and a shrill buzzing in her ears were the last recollections she had before darkness crashed around her.

* * *

Sarah opened her eyes and blinked. Her body was drenched in sweat, and her tongue felt thick and pasty. She dug her fingers into something soft. *Where am I?* She looked around. She was sitting on a thick pink carpet, and Miss Prickle lay by her side. Moonlight streamed through the window and sent a beam of light across the floor. As Sarah reached for her doll, she read the digital printout on her clock radio. It was 11:05 pm.

She stumbled to her feet and sat down on the bed. *My bed! I'm home! I'm safe!* Sarah thought. She squeezed Miss Prickle, threw herself down onto her pink comforter, buried her head in her pillow and smelled the sweet scent of fabric softener on her pillowcase. She looked around. *My desk, my dolls, my trophies, everything's the same!* Sarah thought. She pinched herself and got up slowly.

With Miss Prickle in her arms, she wobbled down the hallway towards her parents' room. A stream of light crept out from under their bedroom door, and she could hear their low voices as they prepared for bed. Sarah barged into their room.

"Mommy, Daddy," she ran over to them and threw her arms around them. She buried her face in between both of them, breathing in their smells, and wrapped herself in the warmth of their bodies before starting to cry.

"What is it, sweetie?" asked her mom. "Are you okay? You're soaking wet."

"I'm fine now." She snuggled in closer. "I thought I would never get back to you."

"Back from where, honey?"

"Back from the past. Miss Prickle and I were gone. We were afraid we would never see you again." Sarah looked from her mother to her father.

"Who's Miss Prickle?" asked her father.

Sarah held up her doll. "She's Miss Prickle. That's what I named her. I hope you're not mad. I know it's not a pretty name."

Louis Osborne let out a laugh. "Of course, I'm not mad. I thought for a while she would go without a name until I got you those roller blades." He messed up his daughter's hair.

"Miss Prickle is better than roller blades any day, Daddy."

"Well, my girl is growing up after all. There's nothing a father can do to keep you little forever."

Sarah looked into her father's soft eyes. "No, you would have to turn back time for that." Sarah kissed both of her parents and walked out of the room. She passed by Jerome's room and peeked in on him. She tiptoed over to his bed and looked down at his peaceful, sleeping face, gently touched his fat little fist, and blew him a kiss.

Sarah returned to her room and rearranged the dolls on her shelves to make room for Miss Prickle. *I should have told them about my...my...my what? Nightmare? No, I've experienced plenty of those before, but none of them have ever seemed so real.* She thought.

Before she placed Miss Prickle on the shelf, she smoothed her dress. There wasn't one wrinkle left in it, and the gift tag on which her father had written *To Sarah, with love* was still in place. The ink hadn't even run from being tossed in the water. *Maybe I just dreamed it. After all, people can't possibly go back in time.* Sarah thought.

Sarah inspected Miss Prickle's cloak and dress one last time and placed her on the top shelf right next to Addie. She looked around her room, drinking in the familiar sights and smells. She walked over to her bookshelf and pulled out her favorite new book, *Brown Girl Dreaming* by Jacqueline Woodson. She ran her fingers along its spine. *Yes, Mr. Hill, I can read,* she thought. *And in my world, a woman of color is quickly becoming a legend for her poetry and stories. So there.* She turned off the light and crawled under the covers.

Sarah lay in bed thinking about her adventure. She tossed and turned with thoughts of Anna, Grandmother, and those dreadful men, Dredge and Hill. She smiled when she remembered Samuel Adams and that pesky, but lovable Culpepper.

Culpepper! That's it! Sarah sprang out of bed, turned on the light and bounded over to Miss Prickle. She opened the tiny red cape, lifted the apron, and then hiked up the doll's dress. Five tiny stitches stretched across Miss Prickle's stomach. Five stitches that Sarah knew were made by the teeth of a small, pesky, yappy dog named Culpepper, in April of the year 1765!

The End

DISCUSSION QUESTIONS FOR SARAH the BOLD

1. How did the author help you understand the setting?
2. What writing technique did the author use to show Sarah's thinking throughout the story?
3. What are some differences between your life and life in the mid-1700s? What are some similarities?
4. If you lived in 1765, would you be a Loyalist or a Patriot? Why?
5. How would you characterize Anna Ruggles? Show evidence from the story.
6. Why do you think the author had Sarah meet Samuel Adams? Do you think it was important to the story? Why or why not?

7. What was Miss Prickle's (the poppet) purpose in the story?
8. Why do you think the author wrote Culpepper (the dog) into the story?
9. How did Sarah change throughout the story?
10. Did you like the ending of the story? What is another way the story could have ended?
11. Which character did you like the most? Why? Which one did you dislike the most? Why?
12. Sarah needed to make a number of choices in this story. Name some and tell which ones you think were wise choices and why you think that.
13. If you could interview one of the characters in the story, which one would you pick? Give an example of a question you would ask that character.
14. Would you recommend this book to a friend? Why or why not?

GLOSSARY OF COLONIAL TERMS FOR READERS OF **SARAH the BOLD**

Anise A licorice-flavored spice that was crushed into a paste and used for toothpaste. Children would put anise paste on a rag and rub it across their teeth to clean them.

Apprentice A person who trains for a trade under the instruction of a master craftsman

Blacksmith A blacksmith is a metalsmith who creates objects from wrought iron or steel by forging the metal, using tools to hammer, bend, and cut

Brown Bess A musket or rifle

Chamber A bedroom

Chamber pot A pot kept next to the bed at night so that people did not need to go outside to use the privy. The pots were emptied in the morning, usually by the children.

Coif A woman's close-fitting cloth cap

Congregation The people who attend a particular church, the word means "to gather together."

Dry sink A basin used for washing with no plumbing system. Used in the days before indoor plumbing

Flogging A whipping, a beating, often in public

Galoshes Boots

Harvest Gathering crops, or the time period for gathering or picking crops

Hoop and Stick Game Hoop rolling, also called hoop trundling, is a child's game in which a large hoop is rolled along the ground, generally by means of a stick wielded by the player. The aim of the game is to keep the hoop upright for long periods of time.

Hymnal A book with songs in it to sing in church

Jack bed Beds much shorter than today's beds, and not long enough to stretch out in and lay straight.

King George III England's longest-ruling monarch before Queen Victoria, King George III (1738-1820) ascended the British throne in 1760. During his 59-year reign, he pushed through a British victory in the Seven Years' War, led England's successful resistance to Revolutionary and Napoleonic France, and presided over the loss of the American Revolution. After suffering intermittent bouts of acute mental illness, he spent his last decade in a fog of insanity and blindness.

Knickers Breeches, pants that came to the knee

Laughingstock Someone whom others make fun of

Lockup A jail

Loom A tool used to weave fabric using yarn or thread

Loyalist A colonist who wished to remain loyal to King George III

Make haste Be quick

Making manners Being polite, girls curtsied and boys bowed.

Meetinghouse A place of worship and for town meetings

Mucking Working manure into garden soil to fertilize it

Parchment A very thin paper made of cloth or linen

Parson A minister

Parsonage The parson's home

Patriot A colonist who wished to break away from the King's rule

Poppet A very simple colonial doll, usually with a wooden or cloth head and cloth body. Some believed poppets had supernatural powers.

Pottage A stew

Privy A toilet located in a small shed outside a house or other building; an outhouse

Quarters Where a person lives

Quill pen A feathered pen that needed to be dipped into an inkwell before it could write. The point of the quill pen was called its nib. Children often needed to sharpen the nibs of the pens for the schoolmaster.

Sabbath House Church goers took a break from their church services to share a meal at the Sabbath house with other churchgoers, and then returned to the meetinghouse for more prayers.

Samuel Adams Founder of the Sons of Liberty

Sarsaparilla A drink similar to root beer

Shipwright Someone who builds and repairs ships

Simone Manuel First African-American woman to win an individual Olympic gold in freestyle swimming and to set an Olympic record and an American record

Snap the Whip A schoolyard game also called Crack the Whip; it involves a line of participants holding hands and being led by the person in front. The object is to make the person holding the other end of the line, fall off. The leader runs a "snaking course" (in any direction that changes fast!) the person on the opposite end is the object to be "thrown off." The line resembles a whip. Thus, the person on the end gets "cracked off."

Sons of Liberty The Sons of Liberty was an organization that was created in the Thirteen American Colonies. The secret society was formed to protect the rights of the colonists and to fight taxation by the British government. They played a major role in most colonies in battling the Stamp Act in 1765. The group officially disbanded after the Stamp Act was repealed.

Spittoon A pot in which men spit tobacco juice or phlegm. It was considered healthier than spitting on the ground or floor.

Stamp Act of 1765 A law that required that many printed materials in the colonies carry an embossed revenue stamp.

Sugar Act of 1764 A law passed by the British Parliament that established a tax on molasses imported by British colonial subjects. It taxed foreign coffee, sugar, pimiento and some wines, and limited the colonists' ability to export lumber and iron to the French West Indies.

Tinsmith Also known as a whitesmith or tinker, it is a person who makes and repairs things made of tin, or other light metals.

Town common A village green, used for animal grazing

Town Watchman Also known as the night watchman, the town watchman guarded the village after dark. No one was allowed to wander around town after dark, or they would be punished. The first colony to use a watchman was Boston in the 1630s.

Trenchers Wooden plates in which to serve food. They had a small well dugout in the middle. Families often shared them with another when there weren't enough to go around.

Trough A long, narrow open container for animals to eat or drink out of

Trundle A bed that had another bed that slid under it. Trundles are still manufactured today.

Udder An udder is an organ formed of the mammary glands of female four-legged mammals, particularly cows, goats, sheep, and deer. It is where their bodies manufacture milk for farmers or to feed their young.

Whipping post A post to which people were tied and whipped in public for their crimes

Yoke A wooden crosspiece that is fastened over the necks of two animals and attached to the plow or cart that they are to pull.

ACKNOWLEDGEMENTS

Numerous friends, colleagues and family members have had a hand in the writing of *Sarah the Bold*, but none so significantly involved as my husband, Larry. He is, and always will be, my alpha reader, my devoted listener, and my True North. He helped me navigate my way through the turbulence and encouraged me to hold my course until I rounded the final buoy. You're the best!

I will always be indebted to the many students who passed through my classroom doors, who inspired me to write this novel and use it as a teaching tool. You guided me with your brilliant questions and comments and became my most candid critique group.

Many thanks to my writing critique groups, the Wallingford Women Writers of Wallingford, Connecticut; the Pamlico Writers' Group of Washington, North

Carolina; and the Madison, Connecticut Chapter of SCBWI. They provided guidance and constructive nudges to help me shape this story into something I am proud of. You will always be my tribe.

My eternal gratitude to Maryann Newsom-Brighton, friend and editor extraordinaire, and proofreader, Mum Linda, who kept me from embarrassing myself publicly by diligently catching my misspellings and grammar mistakes. (I hope you caught them all). And grateful appreciation to Sarah Maury Swan, a friend and fellow writer, who asked the right questions and educated me on farm animals.

Thanks to fellow children authors, Stephanie Robinson and Sarah Maury Swan, for their gracious and kind endorsements of *Sarah the Bold*. You dressed up my back cover.

Special hugs to Nadia Veleas, Annika Veleas and Serena Holmes for taking time out of their busy fifth and sixth-grade schedules to be the best beta readers ever. You rock!

I am indebted to the kind docents of the Henry Whitfield House in Guilford and the Noah Webster House in West Hartford, Connecticut, who answered my numerous questions and never made me feel like a nuisance.

And finally, thank you to the librarians of the Guilford Public Library, who steered me to valuable resources to help me create authentic 1765 Guilford and New Haven town commons for my readers. You made me promise to return when the book was published. It finally is, and I'll be back.

EML

CPSIA information can be obtained
at www.ICGtesting.com
Printed in the USA
LVHW091620300321
682969LV00005B/1037